DEAD
WEIRD

FUNERAL IN GLEN OUTIL, SKYE.

JIM HEWITSON

DEAD WEIRD

BLACK & WHITE PUBLISHING

First published 2004
by Black & White Publishing Ltd
99 Giles Street, Edinburgh EH6 6BZ

ISBN 1 84502 025 1

A CIP catalogue record for this book
is available from The British Library.

Printed and bound by Creative Print and Design

Acknowledgements

Thanks to everyone who talked me through the way Scotland has coped with, and is coping with, death, the greatest adventure of all. Libraries – in particular, Orkney Library, the Mitchell Library in Glasgow, Edinburgh District Library and the Queen Mother Library in Aberdeen – and local authorities across the country, laymen and clergymen alike helped build a picture for me. But my special thanks go out to David MacColl and Dominic Maguire. Their vision of a compassionate future in dealing with death in an increasingly secular world was encouraging.

DEDICATION

In memory of my mum and dad

INTRODUCTION

YOU HAVEN'T LIVED TILL YOU'VE DIED IN SCOTLAND!

Sorry to be the bearer of these tidings but we are all going to snuff it, kick the bucket, shuffle off this mortal coil and cash in our chips. Not to put too fine a point on it – WE ARE ALL GOING TO DIE.

If this stark statement makes you want to put this book back on the shelf and curl up in a corner, then I apologise. I don't mean to offend your sensibilities. And I was well warned by people much wiser than me that attempting an upbeat, animated look at death might bomb spectacularly. Maybe so but this is not a book designed to make you hysterical with fear or fill you with dark despair. It is a genuine attempt to explore, with as light a touch as is reasonable, an everyday experience eventually shared by us all.

This has to be stated clearly at the outset – my impression is that in the second half of the twentieth century, here in Scotland, we were probably more afraid of death, and of those who die, than at any time in our history. When lovers, friends, family, enemies or celebrities took their leave of us, we were confused, uncertain how to respond. Through the media, visions of death and destruction invaded our everyday lives and held us fascinated yet, at the same time, we recoiled at the thought of caring for our own dead.

In an increasingly secular Western world, where, by and large, people live for themselves, where the individual and the cult of youthfulness appears to be all that matters and ideas of community, caring for others, even the concept of family, seem strangely outmoded, we came to look on the traditional rituals of death as not only past their sell-by date but macabre, in bad taste, almost obscene.

I

Those in the know suggest that, in Scotland, a combination of social factors were at work in bringing this situation about. As people were herded out to the new soulless peripheral housing schemes, there was a loss of community solidarity and social cohesiveness. And, since 1948 when the National Health Service came into being, sanitised hospitals have replaced the customary family setting as the most common place for death to occur. The slow drift away from traditional religion – the loss of faith, if you like – also seems to have increased the scariness, the stark finality, of death.

Just along the road from where I'm writing, in the busy heart of Aberdeen, is a funeral parlour. During the cold snaps of the first months of 2004, snow froze on the ground, the Duthie Park looked like Siberian tundra and, if it does not appear too inappropriate and disrespectful to say it, the undertaker's premises at the top of King Street was going like a fair. 'Oh, it always happens at this time of year,' said a friend. 'It's a known fact. Old folk can't handle the cold weather. They die off in droves.'

So we are reminded again of our mortality, of the years creeping by. There is a growing awareness of bad weather, aching bones, poor eyesight and annoying young people who seem too full of vitality. We note the seasons come and go, the trees stretching their green limbs to the sky and then their russet retreat. All around us is beauteous change . . . and decay. This awareness of our mutability and mortality – something, as far as we know, that is unique to the human species and perhaps one of our greatest gifts – should, you might think, by giving us a chance to think on it, lend a tragic dignity to death. Sadly, it seldom does.

II

Most people these days still erect fences whenever conversation turns to death. We all know that we are going to die. The fear, by and large, is not about extinction but about the process of dying – pain, confusion and, of course, sudden death where so many loose ends are left. People are living longer. The nation's health, compared with that of our ancestors, is remarkable – despite an all too frequent diet of burgers, fags and beer. Experts tell me that it is now quite rare for anyone below the age of thirty to have attended a family funeral. The truth is that we are generally ill equipped and gratefully inexperienced at dealing with death.

We work hard to make ourselves immune to the reality of death but this is as difficult as it is pointless. A few stark statistics convey the impossible scale of forgetting. For example, in Britain **EVERY YEAR**, some quarter of a million males alone die. Certainly this total includes the old, wise ones, whose time has come, but also younger folk cut off in their prime – teenagers, even babies. No age grouping is immune. Likewise every year in the United Kingdom 4,000 die in accidents in the home. I was equally staggered to learn that, **EVERY DAY** some 3,000 people die in road accidents across the globe. If, as my fellow Bankie Marti Pellow assures us, 'Love Is All Around', then, most assuredly, so is death.

In all its forms death is with us every living second of the day.

And, to that extent, it is still part of everyday life. However, what has changed in the later twentieth century was our Western way of dealing with death. It was shut out until it could no longer be evaded and then, hurriedly, the rituals were handed over to the specialists – the ministers, the bereavement counsellors, the undertakers, the gravediggers and crematorium operatives.

III

There was a day when the event of death in Scotland was genuinely a part of life – a day for family and community solidarity. It was a day when the person who had passed on was genuinely celebrated in the bosom of the family during the days before his or her burial. This was when friends gathered round the corpse and ate and drank – admittedly, sometimes too freely in the latter case – read the Bible, laughed and cried, remembered the good times and quietly partied. The rituals helped ease the leave-taking. It was one of the basic functions of community. And now it is lost, never likely to return.

In North European societies until the last few years, death was seen as a very private event – free expression of emotion was not encouraged. Generally funerals proceeded in a restrained, quiet and what is seen as a dignified manner. You were discouraged from sharing your grief with the rest of the community. Death was kept at a distance. Advances in medical science had also given rise to the hope that death could be postponed or even avoided and the evidence of increased longevity allowed you to distance yourself from your own death. Thus, when death occurs in Western society, it is now generally outwith the home and involvement of the family is kept to a minimum.

When we look at societies in India, China or even Greece we can see how the Scotland of yesteryear dealt with death. Other cultures do not see life and death as opposing forces but simply as complementary aspects of existence, thus enabling a more level-headed, lighter, familial view of death to be taken.

IV

However, important changes have been identified in Scottish society over the past few years. They seem to be emanating from the cult of the individual. In the words of Thomas Lynch, in his marvellous book about the funeral trade, *The Undertaking*, people at last appear to be getting 'off their ashes'. They seem to be recovering some of their role in giving a proper farewell to their loved ones. Living wills, where the deceased has spelled out in detail just what kind of send-off they expect to have, are now more common.

Dominic Maguire, involved personally in the funeral business in Glasgow for thirty years and the eloquent spokesman for the National Association of Funeral Directors, believes he has identified one important source of this sea change. Many millions on television witnessed the funeral of Diana, Princess of Wales in 1997 and this was an occasion complete with personally relevant music and a distinctly individual feel, rather than the sombre, ritualistic and basically impersonal events to which we had become accustomed. In retrospect, it is being seen as an important cultural watershed.

Never again, unless there is some major social upheaval, will the planning and conduct of funerals be a family/community respons-ibility. When people have the option and the wherewithal to pay someone to do a distasteful job, they will generally seize that opportunity. Undertakers will be kept busy. Nevertheless, the new personalised style and content of funerals, whether religious or secular, are increasingly being designed by loving families, under the watchful, shepherding eye of the undertaker. This phenomenon is being experienced at all social levels. The lives of individual members of the community are being more fully celebrated. It was always thus with VIPs but now, after half a century or more, the day of the honoured, ordinary dead may be returning.

V

This new approach is, of course, not without its dangers. With the 'let's throw a party' style of funeral, there is always the possibility that, amid the theatricals, we still fail to address the issues raised by this final rite of passage. And limits of decency must be set. Funerals where acquaintances tell of the deceased's drunken karaoke exploits in Benidorm as the family sob in the front pew must be avoided.

The way ahead is not easy to predict but it does look as if our relationship with death is undergoing fundamental changes – as it has many times before in our history. Death is certainly still something most of us think about as little as possible. Read what American writer Christine Quigley has to say on the subject. In the same way as the Egyptians at boozy banquets used to wheel in a mummy at the end of the festivities to remind the revellers of their mortality, Christine's chilling summary fair focuses your thoughts:

> Death. The word conveys a threat to each of us.
> One day our heart will cease to beat. One day the electrical
> activity in our brain will draw to a close.

One day we will no longer think, work, play.
We won't even relax as we know it now. Each of us will become a corpse. We will make the transition from animate to inanimate. As a corpse we will not require food, we will not require water and we will not require air. We will, however, require disposal or preservative treatment or we will contaminate the environment of those who continue to live.

VI

But a death is certainly much more than a simple shutting-down of a life system or even a soul taking flight. It is as much about those left behind as it is about the deceased – perhaps more. The cords that bind us stretch beyond death and are strong.

Both my parents are dead – my father in the 1970s, my mother in the 1990s. It is difficult to write about their departure even now. Briefly, my father died at the wheel of his car in Maryhill Road, Glasgow, on his way to work at British Rail's Scottish headquarters and my mother died in a Clydebank nursing home after a stroke. At fifty-eight, my father was a relatively young man by modern standards but he had a weak heart following a bout of scarlet fever as a child which left him with what I have heard doctors call a murmur. He had been taking part in an important World Health Organisation executive screening and had his last all-clear shortly before his death . . . aye, well! My mother, who lived into her eighties, thought she was dying since the 1950s but outlived many of her contemporaries, including her twin sister.

It has to be said that I was not close to my parents. When my father discovered that I had no engineering skills – that, in his words,

I was 'haunless' – I believe he was more disappointed than he would ever admit. I was an only child so perhaps his reaction was understandable. Thankfully, the technical skills of my cousins made up to some extent for my failings.

And I recall, when my wife and I returned home after our long gypsy phase, wandering Europe in a long-wheel base Land Rover, faither dropped his bucket of water as he was washing the car and ran on to Kilbowie Road to meet us. For just a moment, the hard man let his guard down.

VII

My mother relied totally on my father for everything and her first words to me within minutes of my father's sudden death are etched in my mind. 'Who's going to look after me now?' she enquired. Of course, I promised I would. But, truth to tell, I did not make much of a job of it. When we moved away from Central Scotland, my mother would not come with us. She wanted to stay in Clydebank among the places and faces with which she was familiar. However, she was becoming less and less capable of looking after herself. A crisis was inevitable in months rather than years. So I 'persuaded' her to go into a nursing home, first of all in Helensburgh and then in Clydebank. For much of that time – and in the end it amounted to ten years – either in our phone calls or very occasional visits, she gave me the impression that she was living a miserable life. Friends and family told me otherwise but that was how she presented her life to me. And cash from my father's forty years of hard graft in the railways steadily evaporated meeting my mother's monthly accommodation bill. Guilt? Tell me about it.

These thoughts are just a preamble to a couple of observations about seeing off my parents. With my old pal Alan MacDermid as a witness, I formally identified my father on the mortuary slab in the Saltmarket. He had died on a public road, you see. Formalities. Formalities. As I looked at his shell, his cocoon – for, wherever my father was by that time, he was not around in the Saltmarket – stretched beneath a plastic sheet on the shiny metal table, I recalled the only real piece of wisdom which he ever imparted to me. 'What's for ye, will no' go past ye, son,' he said. The older I get, the more I tend to believe that.

VIII

And my mother . . . well, her ashes lie in Cadder Cemetery on the northern outskirts of Glasgow, not cosily beside my father as she wanted but about thirty yards away in another lair. Yes, 'haunless' Jim here, who had successfully screwed up the later years of her life, or so she told me, managed to put her in the wrong grave! The Hewitson family had two plots and, in the confusion in the aftermath of her death, I mixed up the documents. As we laid her to rest, I thought there was something unfamiliar about the location. The cost and complications of having her moved again were daunting. I like to believe they both would have wanted their grandchildren to benefit from the cash that paying for a move would have entailed. I wonder if I'll ever know.

And yet I often heard both of them say that everybody needs a bit of time and space to themselves. The truth is that my mum and dad will spend eternity within comfortable shouting distance of each other. Laugh in the face of death, whit me?

So, this book, although occasionally ranging across the globe, is about death, the Scots and the Caledonian take on the last great adventure. It is about the way we die and have died, about the official taking of life through execution, murder and mayhem, traditions and oddities, hints of the other world, legends and lists. It is also about the frothy side of death. Yes, there is a frothy, even funny, side to death. My original reticence in tackling this book project in an airy way vanished when I discovered that laughter therapy, if we can call it that, is now regarded as crucial in the care of the terminally ill. At its simplest level, this may just be sitting, holding someone's hand and sharing memories of the sad, bad old days. Death truly is a part of our life.

IX

Laughter can help us cope with the death of friends and family and ease the stress surrounding grief. Freud put it this way – 'humour can act as a defence mechanism against unpleasure'. It can reach out to the terminally ill, destroy the 'them and us' syndrome, the gulf between the dying and those caring for the terminally ill, and offer a truly shared experience. Even more importantly, it can provide a safety valve for our anxieties about death. What then is more appropriate, after expressing wonder, awe and bafflement over the final farewell, than to laugh, or at least chuckle, in the face of death itself? Existence demands no less of our species that has the unique ability to reflect on this wonderful life and the possibilities that lie beyond.

Jim Hewitson, Papa Westray

ACCEPTANCE

When James Boswell, the eighteenth-century Scottish travelling buddy of the illustrious Dr Samuel Johnson, tried to draw out the great man's thoughts on eternity, he got instead short shrift. In his *Life of Johnson*, Boswell highlights the moment when their extensive conversations turned briefly to the topic of death. Boswell records:

> To my question, whether or not we might fortify our minds for the approach of death, he answered, in a passion: 'No, Sir, let it alone. It matters not how a man dies, but how he lives. The act of dying is not of importance, it lasts so short a time.'

It seems likely that at least some of the Johnsonian philosophy may have been gleaned from the Bard of Avon:

> Of all the wonders that I have yet heard,
> It seems most strange to me that men should fear,
> Seeing that death, a necessary end,
> Will come when it will come.
>
> *Julius Caesar*, Act II, Scene 2

11

However, our own Robert Louis Stevenson summed up this quiet acceptance that things will be as they will be in his classic 'Requiem', the last two lines of which are found on his tomb in the South Pacific:

Under the wide and starry sky,
Dig my grave and let me lie:
Glad did I live and gladly die,
And I laid me down with a will.

This be the verse you 'grave for me:
Here he lies where he long'd to be;
Home is the sailor, home from the sea,
And the hunter home from the hill.

ACCIDENTAL DEATH

After William of Orange died in a riding accident in 1702 when his horse stumbled in a molehill, cocky Scots Jacobites got into the habit of discretely toasting 'the wee gentleman in the velvet jacket'.

ACCOUNTS

The bill for expenses at the funeral of a northern laird – Sir Hugh Campbell of Calder, who died in March 1716 – gives some idea of the extent of hospitality at such events in the eighteenth century. There was a charge of £55 15s 'to buy ane cow, ane ox, five kids, two wedders, eggs, geese, turkeys, pigs and moorfowl'. Besides £40 for brandy to John Finlay in Forres, £25 4s for claret to John Roy in Forres, £82 6s to Bailie Cattenach at Aberdeen for claret and £35 to John Fraser in Clunas for 'waters' (i.e. whisky), there was a huge food bill and, all told, the cost was reckoned at £1,647 16s 4d. This, the chronicler tells us, represented a 'comparatively moderate' funeral for a man of such eminence and to get an idea of how much the toffs spent all the figures should be multiplied by three.

Twentieth-century preacher and social commentator Henry Gray Graham remarked of the eighteenth century in Scotland that it was 'dangerous to be ill, an expensive thing to die and a ruinous thing to be buried'.

The ruin really only threatened those who had wherewithal to waste on an extravagant send-off for the deceased. Evidence of this can be found aplenty in the parish records. In the early 1800s, it cost £30 12s – a huge sum in today's terms – to bury the minister at Balfron in Stirlingshire. This sum included over £12 for rum, wine and brandy and, wait for it, 24s for shortbread. Death really was a luxury beyond the reach of the poor.

ACTORS AND ACTRESSES

One of the most colourful characters in the Perthshire community of Errol in the mid 1800s was 'Fizzie' Gow. A tailor to trade and a showman by nature, he was also part-time town crier. He was undaunted in presenting performances of such classics as Shakespeare's *Macbeth*. His wife generally acted with him and was famous for her 'dying' roles. In response to continuous applause following his missus's dramatic 'departures', Gow would announce solemnly, in his peculiar 'fizzing' speech, that his wife would happily 'diesh againsh' to please such an enthusiastic audience. And she did!

The famous Australian opera singer Dame Nellie Melba, born Helen Porter Mitchell, daughter of an emigrant Scots builder David Mitchell, always had a healthy contempt for the presence of the grim reaper. While touring the United States in *Othello*, she played Desdemona with such passion that women in the audience were seen to burst into floods of tears as she was strangled by Othello. If the applause persisted she would rise miraculously from her death bed, signal for a piano to be trundled on to the stage and she would then accompany herself and sing 'Home Sweet Home' with the enthusiastic audience joining in the chorus. When the ovation ceased, she would collapse again and allow Othello to finish the job.

ADVANCE WARNING

The rhythmic scrape of the coffin maker's plane was often said to have been heard in Highland clachans the night before his services were actually required. Whether this was as a result of some eerie ability to see into the future, as some suggest, or just a very practical knowledge about which of his neighbours was nearing the end of the road, we can only guess.

ADVERTISING

The fact that hearses were in use in the cities of Scotland, around the time of the Union with England, is confirmed by this advert from the *Edinburgh Courant* of 13 May 1707:

This is to give notice to all who have occasion for a black hersse, murning-coach, and other coaches, just new, and in good order, with good horses well accoutred, that James Mouat, coachmaster in Lawrence Ord's Land at the foot of the Canongate, will serve them thankfully and at reasonable rates.

While professional undertakers began to flourish in the cities and towns, the transport of the deceased in rural areas could be much more problematical. Every form of conveyance from manure cairt to milk float was employed to take folk to their last resting place.

AGE

† Auld men will die and bairns will sune forget
† Auld Highland Games wrestlers dinna die, they just lose their grip on life
† Auld Clyde yachtsmen never die, they just keel over

The dubious honour of being the oldest recorded Scottish and possibly European victim of a full-scale battle falls to the veteran scrapper Maitland of Lethington, father of Sir Richard Maitland, the poet, lawyer and statesman. Records show that, when the old-timer was slain on the bloody field of Flodden in 1513, he was said to be in his ninetieth year.

AMERICAN WAY OF DEATH

Yanks – don't you just love them? One long-term observer of American funerals noted widely varying reactions to the event among his friends and relatives over the years. He had seen weird practices such as feeding popcorn to the children to keep them quiet and relatives screaming, kicking the coffin and jumping into the grave. At other funerals, however, the ceremony was conducted amid the strictest silence and with the most profound decorum.

The phraseology of death in the American funeral business, as you would expect, is also a wee bit special. How long will it be before we find inspirational gems etched on gravestones along the lines of the following?

† Not Deceased, Dimensionally Challenged
† I'm Not Dead, I've Simply Awakened the Dead Person
  Within Me

It'll come, mark my words.

According to Buck Wolf of the ABC news network, Americans are also constantly attempting to increase the 'fun' at funerals. Could it be that, just occasionally, in their enthusiasm, they are showing the same lack of restraint, good taste and dignity that characterises everything they do from food to fashion?

It was reported by a funeral company in Indiana that one dear departed had commissioned a group of exotic dancers for his funeral while another was buried with his favourite golf club – a Callaway Big Bertha driver, apparently. Bizarre themed funerals are on the increase with one West Coast parlour having been kitted out like a boxing ring for the funeral of a fight fan, complete with a drop-down microphone through which mourners delivered eulogies. Jazz funerals are also popular, as are huntin'/shootin' farewells with the funeral parlour decked out like a hunting lodge.

It seems clear that this is an attempt to recreate the public persona of the deceased in their most familiar form. When funerals were held in a religious context amid people and the objects that gave meaning to the life of the individual, this was not really so necessary. Considering the natural development of such bizarre behaviour, Wolf conjures up the picture of the couch-potato sports fan being buried with his can of beer, packet of cheese and onion crisps and the TV remote control. It might happen – it probably already has happened.

That the United States is a nation that even attempts to inject a bit of fun into the event of death itself should come as no surprise. On one occasion, a San Francisco radio station offered a crate of drink to the family of the 1000th person to die by jumping off the Golden Gate Bridge.

Nor are the common-sense folk of Canada exempt from this nonsense. In Sault Ste Marie, Ontario, the funeral of a dairy farmer featured, as its star attraction, a life-size plastic cow which the deceased had kept on his front lawn and which he moved around daily to give the impression that it was grazing. Straw bales and farmyard fencing were introduced to the funeral parlour to give that extra touch of authenticity.

Hopefully, in Scotland, we are not ready, and never will be, for such bizarre, tasteless, extreme theatricals on the edge of eternity. Fun's fun, as they say, but let's keep some sort of sense of proportion.

AMONG THE SUITCASES

Airlines do not trumpet the fact that an interestingly high proportion of their passengers are now actually housed in the baggage compartment – jet-setting deceaseds heading for their final landing.

ANATOMY

After flourishing during ancient Greek and Roman times, the study of anatomy resumed during the Renaissance. However, the availability of cadavers was restricted by law. In the 1600s, Edinburgh town council gave the city's surgeons the authority to use the body of one executed criminal every year and they were also permitted to study those of foundlings or stillbirths.

ANIMALS

A death in the family was always a sign to lock up domestic pets. Apart from being a bittie undignified it was considered an omen of desperate misfortune if the cat or dog jumped across or on top of the deceased. In certain parts of the country, according to Anne Gordon, author of the definitive academic work on Scottish burial customs, *Death is for the Living*, the belief was that the first person to see an animal that had done so would lose their sight.

Bullfighting is generally regarded as one of the bloodiest public death sports the world still has to offer. This is particularly ironic because the home of the matador, Spain, is also the country that believes its people to be so squeamish that they should not be allowed to view television programmes about the best way to handle terminal illness.

APOLOGIES

There is a bizarre story of the final seconds in the life of Aberdonian adventurer Alexander Blackwell who was executed in Sweden for alleged involvement in a plot against the royal family. Apparently, when he bent to place his head on the block, he had approached from the wrong side and was duly corrected by the executioner who guided Blackwell into the proper position. His last words were reportedly, 'I'm sorry for the mistake. This is the first time I've been beheaded.'

ASH

In Greenock they still remember the day it snowed white ash but this wasn't fall-out from some distant volcano. One of the customers of a local undertaker was an old soldier. He had lost his leg in the Second World War and, in order to balance the coffin for carrying it to the cremation, it was decided to fill the vacant corner of the box with old newspapers. A memorable blaze was produced.

ASSASSINATION

Glasgow-born Allan Pinkerton emigrated to the United States and founded the famous detective agency named after him. He confessed that his greatest challenge – and failure – had been in trying to persuade the ill-fated US President Abe Lincoln that he was in danger of assassination. Lincoln, of course, was shot in 1865 while at the theatre.

The world's first televised assassination happened in 1960 in Japan when Inejiro Asanuma, chairman of the Japanese Socialist Party, was gutted with a sword by a political activist.

ASYLUM SEEKERS

The most unusual occupant of Kenmore Kirkyard in Perthshire is the infant son of the former ruler of the Punjab, Maharajah Duleep Singh. Having been exiled in Victorian Britain, the Maharajah was, like his Queen, an enthusiast for all things Scottish and spent holidays beside Loch Tay. During one of these visits, his son died and found his final resting place under Scottish soil – a little corner of Perthshire that is forever the Punjab.

AVIATION

The advent of jet aircraft, which could speed Scottish funeral directors across the Atlantic to see what their American and Canadian cousins were up to, resulted in the funeral business in Scotland, from the 1960s onwards, being awash with ideas about embalming, funeral parlours and rest rooms. The idea of cremation also began to gather wider acceptance as a result of this increased air travel.

AVOIDING DEATH

A straw poll of that dwindling band of folk, Scottish churchgoers, would surely nominate the twenty-third psalm ('The Lord's My Shepherd') as the big all-time favourite, particularly for funerals. I would plead the case of Psalm 119 – if only because of its remarkable life-giving properties. Apart from its poetic radiance and its spiritual appeal, this psalm also just happens to be the longest, extending to over 350 lines.

When one of the Marquis of Montrose's chaplains was sentenced to death for his part in his master's exploits, he pinned his faith in the Lord, always believing that he would be reprieved. Even as he was being led out to the gallows in Edinburgh and the ladder was set in place, he remained confident of a pardon.

It was the custom, in the seventeenth century, for a condemned man to be asked to choose which psalm was to be read. Now, if you're in such a situation and desperate to get things over and done with, with the minimum of fuss, then Psalm 117 is the one for you – all twenty-four words of it. There would be no hanging about with that one – if you'll pardon the pun. But the shrewd clergyman, convinced of the merits of procrastination, chose Psalm 119. Before it was three-quarters complete, eyewitnesses related that a reprieve came and he was spared the noose.

BAKING

When MacDougall, a Highland baker, went to that great pie shop in the sky, his community was devastated. No longer would they be blessed with his epic buns. To no one's surprise, the funeral took place at 450 for about 20 minutes.

BEANFEST

Galloway's notorious cannibal family the Beans are thought to have killed, barbecued and consumed up to 1,000 passers-by in their roadside pied-à-terre.

BEGGARS — STURDY AND OTHERWISE

Every beggar and spring-heeled musician on the streets of Glasgow in the 1950s had a limousine waiting around the corner ready to speed him home to his luxurious south-side apartment. This folk myth, whispered to me by someone older and seemingly wiser when

I still sported short trousers and an open mind, haunted me for years.

'Look at the hands, son, look at the hands. Never done a day's work in their life,' confided the wise one. It wasn't until I completed a few nightshifts as a reporter on calls in the city centre that this fib was fully and finally exploded. The truth is that homelessness, squalor, despair and death are the customary lot of the modern beggar and the only view of the world from an automobile that they are likely to experience is from the back of a police van.

But, just occasionally, I still come across a story that fuels the myth of the wealthy beggar. In 1817, William Stevenson of Kilmarnock died. Although trained as a mason, he spent the greater part of his life, up until he was in his eighties, as a beggar. He was seized by an incurable illness and, a few days before his death, he began to spend, spend, spend. Astonished friends saw the baker summoned and ordered to produce twelve dozen burial cakes and a large quantity of sugared biscuits. A good supply of wines and spirits was also ordered up. Stevenson arranged for the construction of a sound, dry, roomy, comfortable and expensive coffin and the same meticulous attention was paid to the digging of the grave in the churchyard at Riccarton.

After his death, neighbours found a bagful of silver pieces, bonds and other money. Eventually a staggering total of about £1,000 was brought to light. His will set aside money for a funeral feast for the beggar fraternity who came from far and near for the send-off. A barn was fitted up for the occasion and, at this remarkable beggars' banquet, the revelries that took place were said to be 'little in accordance with the season of death'. And the toast was 'Guid auld Wullie!'

BELIEF

We'd all like to think there was a life after death – but belief can be a confusing thing. It is better to believe in something that isn't than not to believe in something that is. So declared the clever seventeenth-century French scholar Blaise Pascal. I'm sure Blaise knew exactly what he was on about – but I'm damned if I do.

BELLS

In the century after the Reformation, some strict elders in the kirk saw bells as a relic of popery but, by the late 1600s, no parish church in Scotland was complete without its bell. All across the country there were wee thatched kirks without belfries so the bell was fixed into the wall by an iron support or hung on a nearby tree.

The 'dead' bell or mortbell was used either to announce the passing of one of the local inhabitants or to summon the community to a funeral. In April 1735, Paisley Town Council appointed Robert White, cow-owner, to 'go with the dead bell', meaning that he should go round the town ringing the dead bell whenever there was a bereavement. The bell was an important feature of every funeral, whether it was carried with the coffin to the grave or rung at the kirk. And the church jealously guarded its right not only to ring the bells but also to charge for the privilege. In fact, even those who still saw the bells as a papist throwback realised that ringing at funerals could provide revenue to help the poor or upgrade a crumbling kirk.

In the 1700s, the kirk session at Invera'an in Strathspey was reported as having been upset at the way in which 'a great many people got up and rang the bell at burials without permission and

24

without paying for the privilege'. They declared that, in future, anyone doing so would be liable to prosecution. However, paying for the bell to be tolled during a funeral clearly remained a matter of some controversy. In the parish of Glamis in 1741, a half-merk charge which had been imposed for the bell to be rung at funerals was described as 'ill-judged' and was withdrawn.

The unexpected tolling of a church bell was often seen as an omen of impending death. One night in the 1600s at Dunblane, the cathedral bell began to clang ferociously. Looking into the building, the beadle could just about make out a mad dark visage and hoofed feet. The elders were convinced that Auld Nick was in their midst and summoned the minister, who arrived, armed only with his bible, to tackle the Prince of Darkness, the Earl of Hell, Auld Clootie. He marched into the cathedral ready to face man's greatest enemy only to find that a practical joker had tied the bell-rope to the horns of a blackface ram who, in his strenuous efforts to escape, had set the bell ringing good style.

By all accounts, the town's hand-held funeral bell was an extra-special specimen with a seventeenth-century date and the initials SB for St Blane stamped on it. The bell was five inches deep with a five-and-a-half-inch handle. On one occasion, it was stolen by a drunken tramp who made the mistake of joyously ringing it as he staggered down the High Street.

BEST SHROUD AND TUCKER

Increasingly, undertakers in Scotland are noting that, as part of the new cult of personalised funerals, people are being buried or cremated in the gear with which they were most comfortable in life.

You can't help but think of this as a healthy trend. After all, who wants to head off into eternity looking like a tailor's dummy? Here are the top choices for going-away gear:

† Coolest suit (men and women)
† Pyjamas (with our without alarm clock!)
† Graduation gown
† Football/rugby strip
† Wedding/confirmation dress
† Clown suit
† Military uniform
† Favourite T-shirt
† Country and western gear
† Masonic outfit

However, it's not just the deceased who are dressing down for eternity. One of the most dramatic changes in funeral behaviour over recent years has been the move away from mourners wearing black ties and Sunday best at funerals. There is now no problem paying your last respects wearing bright colours or jeans.

BIBLE REFERENCES TO DEATH BELOVED BY SOMBRE SCOTS

Sometimes it's very easy to imagine that the Scots are, as some suggest, the Lost Tribe of Israel. So much of the sombre stuff in the Bible, particularly the Old Testament rings a bell, a mortbell no doubt, within the Scottish psyche. Then again, perhaps we should thank John Knox and his gang for giving us the heebie-jeebies.

And I looked, and behold a pale horse: and his name that sat on him was Death and Hell followed with him.

Revelation 6.8 (beloved by Scots and Clint Eastwood fans)

To be carnally-minded is death.

Romans 8.6 (you've been warned!)

Be thou faithful unto death, and I will give thee a crown of life.

Revelations 2.10

O Death where is thy sting? O Grave where is thy victory?

I Corinthians 15.55

The people that walked in darkness have seen a great light: they that dwell in the land of the shadow of death, upon them the light hath shined.

Isaiah 9.2

We have made a covenant with death, and with hell we are at agreement.

Isaiah 28.15 (a personal favourite!)

The last enemy that shall be destroyed is death.

I Corinthians 15.26

He will swallow up death in victory; and the Lord God will wipe away tears from off all faces.

Isaiah 25.8

27

BILLS

It was, of course, the duty of relatives to ensure that those who attended a funeral were well supplied with food and drink and properly entertained. This, quite naturally, resulted in family disputes. From Dunfermline in 1761 surfaces a letter from one brother to another, presumably following the death of one of their parents. The recipient lived away from home and had been unable to attend the funeral.

The letter-writer pointedly says:

> We had plenty of ale, whisky and brandy, and plain and sugared shortbread – and I have paid all funeral expenses.

Clearly bro was now expected to cough up his share of the bill.

BIRDS

There is a strange anomaly in relation to birds as fatal omens. The raven and the crow are the birdies seen most often as omens of death. However, an old Scottish rhyme runs:

> One magpie's joy,
> Two's grief,
> Three's a marriage,
> Four's a death.

In Scotland, according to Colin Walker, author of *Scottish Proverbs*, one magpie, as above, was very much a positive sighting whereas, in England, strangely, it was regarded as a harbinger of sorrow. Grief was a commonplace experience in Scotland of yore so, not surprisingly, a pair of magpies was also a common sight.

An t-eun sith is a mysterious bird of the Scottish Gaelic tradition which haunts the house where a death is set to take place or near a person about to die. It is of indeterminate origin.

The way in which the natural world can hint that the transition between life and death may not be the great chasm, the inconceivable change, that we imagine is well illustrated in three beautiful lines from Kato Shuson:

A winter seagull
In its life has no home
In its death no grave.

In Gaelic culture, a cock crowing before midnight was held to be a sign of approaching news. To flesh out the detail of that news you were obliged to grip the cock and feel its legs – if they were cold to the touch, the news would be of death.

BIZARRE DEATHS

However, bizarre deaths aplenty are found throughout history. Horace Wells, who pioneered the use of anaesthesia, committed suicide while anaesthetised with chloroform. Attila the Hun died of a nosebleed. Astronomer Tycho Brahe's bladder exploded. The

Greek playwright Aeschylus was killed by a falling tortoise. And the man who sparked the jogging craze, Jim Fixx, died while out running.

BLACK HUMOUR

Poking fun at such a serious subject as death has more than once been described poetically as the 'hiss of the safety valve on the pressure cooker'.

BLASPHEMY

Death sentences were handed out to Scottish 'criminals' in centuries past for all sorts of bizarre offences from stealing a piece of linen from a bleachfield to having too close a relationship with an attractive mare.

One of the most appalling must surely be the execution in 1696 of eighteen-year-old student Thomas Aikenhead for the 'crime' of blasphemy. Among other transgressions, young Aikenhead had apparently got into the habit of speaking of theology as 'a rhapsody of feigned and ill-invented nonsense'. He also referred to 'that Impostor Christ' and was charged with claiming that God, the world and nature were 'but one thing, and that the world was from eternity'. Most damningly, he expressed the hope that he would live to see Christianity greatly weakened.

When he saw the force of the Scottish establishment – church and judiciary – ranged against him, Aikenhead issued a petition of retraction in which he pleaded youthful innocence, saying he had only repeated objectionable expressions that he had read and he certainly did not originate them. When you consider some of the poetic nature of the blasphemy, this plea does have a ring of authenticity.

The church does not come well out of this affair. It does look as if they were after the young blasphemer's blood. When Aikenhead was reconciled to his fate, he asked for a brief reprieve to be reconciled to God. However, the Kirk was having none of it.

As his execution day approached he penned a last letter in which he described his education and the earnest hope that his death might stem the tide of atheism and blasphemy which was sweeping the country. The last moments of this unhappy young man are described thus:

> He walked thither to the place of execution a mile from the prison on foot, between a strong guard of fusiliers drawn up in two lines. Several ministers attended him in his last moments and, according to all human appearance, he died with all the marks of a true penitent.

Aikenhead was buried at the foot of the gallows on the road between Leith and Edinburgh. It is a fact that the three principal witnesses who were responsible for his conviction were fellow students.

BOATS

In his research, Orkney folklorist Ernest Marwick refers to a strange belief among the fishermen of the Northern Isles that they would remain alive as long as their boat was intact. Orcadian poet Robert Rendall remembered this tradition:

Both man and boat, meebe, in spite of weather,
For twa'r three winters yet'll haad together.

Strangely, during my years on Papa Westray, there was an old beached fishing boat on the east shore which inexplicably appeared to be holding out against time and tide. Suddenly it began to deteriorate and, within a few months, its owner, Johnny Rendall, was dead.

In Shetland, it was known for old fishermen to carry out repairs on boats that would never sail again, simply to guarantee themselves a few extra years. In fishing communities, particularly in the Northeast, people believed that the spirit of the dead person would await the first outgoing tide before bidding farewell to the community where it had been nurtured.

There are normally about twenty burials at sea annually in United Kingdom waters. Not all of these go without a hitch and the sight of bobbing coffins that simply refused to sink as the weight within shifted has caused distress to relatives and embarrassment to funeral organisers.

BODIES

Simon Fraser, Lord Lovat was the last man to be executed in Britain with an axe. A nobleman who changed sides, from Jacobite rebel to government supporter, like the wind changes direction, Lovat was beheaded on London's Tower Hill on 9 April 1747. His departure was filled with controversy – and mystery.

† He had requested permission to be executed by the Scottish

Maiden, our very own guillotine, in Edinburgh, but this was refused.

† He was struggling to climb the scaffold on the day of his execution – being in his eightieth year – and was helped up the steps to his appointment with the axeman.

† When a stand collapsed during the execution on Tower Hill, twenty people were killed.

† As he was led to his death he expressed disbelief that such a vast crowd should have gathered to witness the 'taking off of an old grey head'.

† A local undertaker had agreed to take the body back to Scotland secretly. But, before doing so, he put the old Jacobite on display in his funeral parlour and charged admission to view the body.

† Officially the body was returned for burial in the Tower of London but the Lovat family has claimed that his remains are in the family tomb at Kirkhill, Inverness.

BODYSNATCHERS

Grave robbers, resurrectionists, bodysnatchers . . . in the first half of the nineteenth century the trade in human corpses for anatomy classes at the world-renowned Scottish schools of medicine was extensive. Bodies preserved in brine were even imported from Ireland.

The punishment for William Burke, the Edinburgh bodysnatcher-turned-murderer, was fitting. After he was executed in 1829 in front of a crowd of 20,000, Burke was publicly dissected in the anatomy lecture theatre on the same slab where some of his victims had ended up. Tickets to the anatomy demonstration were distributed to important citizens and outstanding medical students. The fact that not all the city's students were invited to attend prompted 2000 of them to riot until they were given permission to view the corpse. The general public were also allowed to file past the partly dissected body the following day and as many as 40,000 citizens did so. It is said that Burke's skin was tanned after dissection and sold for a shilling an inch. His skeleton still hangs in the Anatomy Museum of the University of Edinburgh.

Iron coffins came into use from the late 1700s in Scotland in an effort to fox the 'resurrection men'. A patent for this style of coffin is recorded in 1796.

In the absence of these lockfast metal caskets, grave watchers were employed. Such a 'watching' contract was found in the accounts of the Duff family. They forked out £2 4s for having the graves of General Patrick Duff of Carnoustie and his wife in Greyfriars Churchyard, Edinburgh, watched.

Mortsafes were also used to deter the grave robbers. These were heavy iron frames which were fixed over the coffins.

Many families, anxious to protect the eternal slumber of their kinsfolk from bodysnatchers, even set gun-traps, operated by trip wires, along dark paths in the graveyards. Several would-be bodysnatchers were killed by this technique and many injured.

Protection from grave robbers was only thought necessary for a period of six or seven weeks. After that, the corpse would have deteriorated to such an extent that it would no longer be of use for the anatomy table – as Robert Henderson observes in *Scottish Keeriosities*, the body, by this time, had lost its commercial value.

Near my former home in Inverurie, at the kirkyard of Udny, is one of Scotland's most unusual morthouses or lockfast chambers. Here corpses were stored until they were no longer of interest to the grave robbers. The building is circular and inside there is a turntable on which the coffins were placed in sequence. Every time a new corpse was laid on it, the turntable was moved forward a notch and by the time the corpse had completed a circuit it was reckoned to be rotted well beyond 'resurrecting' and could safely be given a proper burial.

In the 1820s, the community in Dunblane in Perthshire was much troubled by the activities of the resurrectionists. A watch was established in the kirkyard, the guard patrolling with lantern and cudgel in hand. The night watchmen had their guardhouse in a little apartment in the west gable of the cathedral. In the parish records in an entry for 8 June 1828, reference is made to what may have been the last case of its kind in the district. It seems that the congregation knew who the bodysnatchers were but, when the procurator fiscal asked for the names of the informants in order to question them, the session clerk declared that the names of the grave robbers were a matter of public notoriety and it was up to the fiscal to trace the villains himself. Perhaps unsurprisingly this was the last we hear of this case but it does make you wonder how often such an impasse was reached across the country. Anatomy schools were finally licensed by the 1832 Anatomy Act which clarified the rules on body supply.

BONES (BARE)

Edward I (1239–1307) detested the Scots who refused to fall in line as his dutiful serfs. You must remember his imagined utterance in *Braveheart* – 'The only trouble with Scotland is that it's full of Scots.', a sentiment occasionally echoed by our southern neighbours. You may not be surprised, therefore, to learn that, on his deathbed, while campaigning against his old adversaries, Edward asked for his corpse to be boiled and the flesh stripped so that his bones could be carted around on future campaigns against the rebellious Caledonians. Even his liegemen thought this a trifle eccentric and his wish was never carried out.

Universities place special importance on the regalia and relics produced for occasions of pomp and ceremony. In its early years, however, poor old Edinburgh University could only boast a modest mace and the skull of George Buchanan, tutor to James VI, for their big days.

BOUNDARIES

Skeabost River on Skye marked the borderline between the lands of the MacDonalds and the MacLeods. Not far from its mouth, the river breaks into two streams. The two burns then rejoin and so an island is formed. Both clans claimed this island was theirs and a long and bloody battle was fought where a huge cairn now stands. After the fighting a truce was called and it was agreed that the disputed island should be made into a burial place, common to both clans. The dead were heaped together and the cairn built over them. Pity there was no one wise enough to offer this way out before the blood was spilled.

BURIAL

The Romans buried their dead but the ancient Greeks had the option of either burning or burying theirs. Until Christianity began to

Iona Abbey

spread, the burning of bodies was common. The ceremony of burial probably became general by the beginning of the fifth century AD but it wasn't until the arrival of the Norman nobility in Scotland in the twelfth century that graveyards – encircling churches and chapels – began to develop.

John MacCodrum, the Uist bard, represents bardic wit at its sharpest and yet most subtle. On one occasion, he paid a visit to his friend Flora Macdonald, the heroine of the Forty-Five, at her home at Kingsburgh. On his arrival, he was unrecognised by one of the maids who showed him into the kitchen. 'And where did you come from?' asked the maid brusquely.

'From Uist,' John responded.

'Is it true that Clanranald is dead?' the maid inquired.

'If not,' said John, 'a great crime has been committed.'

'How is that?' said the uppity maid.

'Well, they buried him a fortnight ago,' said MacCodrum.

The two most popular burial grounds for Scottish monarchs are at the ancient abbey on Iona, where royal burials took place until 1098, and Dunfermline Abbey, where sixteen Scottish rulers have been laid to rest.

BURNING ISSUE

Local authorities occasionally have more than one environmental facility at their crematorium sites. At a West of Scotland crematorium, this included a plant for the recycling of waste paper. The elderly mother of a foreman based there used to carefully wrap up her newspapers and set them by the front door for her son to collect and take down to the crematorium. When the recycling unit was relocated and the foreman told his mother that the paper was no longer needed, she was perplexed and concerned. She asked, 'How are you going to get the cremator started without all my papers?'

CAIRNS

Throughout the Highlands, as well as countless rocky mounds created by natural rockfalls, there are hundreds of cairns. These were erected to mark battlefields and places of individual tragedies. Originally, the stones would have been piled on the deceased but, over the centuries, the cairns were preserved by passers-by adding stones as a mark of respect for the dead. It was considered not only ill-mannered not to add your own tribute in passing but also to be an act of folly that was likely to bring with it decidedly bad luck.

Among the many other cairns on Skye are two beside Loch Curcusdal which tell a particularly sad story – a double tragedy which overtook a winter bridal party. In the early 1800s, the group, which was comprised of the bridegroom, two friends, the bride and her sister, had crossed the hill to Snizort to go and visit friends. On the return leg, the bridegroom became ill. Although helped along by his friends, he died beside the loch, above Maligar. Night fell, it was pitch dark and, to add to their difficulties, snow and mist obscured all the contours of the landscape. It was agreed that the two women should press on for help. A swollen stream forced a long deviation and, as the hours passed, the remaining watchers by the body took a decision. One would remain with the corpse and the other, Lachlan Martin of Marrishader, should also set off to seek help.

The women ultimately reached safety but, because of the darkness, nothing could be done until morning. When the rescue party got to the scene, they found they had two corpses to collect. Martin's remains were found on the opposite bank of the loch. He seems to have stumbled, fallen into the loch and eventually emerged from the water. Lying drenched on the loch shore, he froze to death. Cairns mark the locations where the bridegroom and his unfortunate friend Martin perished. Although it's not clear whether the first wedding ever actually took place, one positive outcome was that the bride went on to marry and live a long and fruitful life.

Resting cairns were of a different category altogether. They were constructed along the route funeral parties would take to the graveyard. This type of cairn was known in Gaelic as a *suidhe*, literally a 'seat'. In Orkney and Shetland, they are called wheelie-stanes. One of the most noted burial places in the West Highlands is Eilean Fhianian, which served the whole of Moidart, Sunart and the nearer parts of Morvern and Ardnamurchan. All roads led to this little island and the 'ways of the dead' are marked, literally, by hundreds of resting cairns. This ancient practice, which is found all over the world, transcended religious changes in Scotland.

There may, however, have been much more subtle reasons for the construction of the cairn. Irish Gaels certainly believed that a place touched by death would grow 'malign and hungry grass' thereafter. Cairns can also represent memorials to people lost at sea and they sometimes mark the site of a murder or the spot where people were killed in a Viking raid or a clan feud.

41

Death candles were a strange warning of impending tragedy in the Scotland of yesteryear and one area where they seem to have been prevalent was in darkest Perthshire. At Crieff one evening, a local man, Robert Armstrong, doing what most countryfolk do, stepped out of his front door in the gloaming to smell the weather and look at the sky. He saw a light crossing a nearby bridge and waited to see who was passing by. As the light approached, he realised he could hear no footsteps and, when the light stopped directly in front of him, he dived inside and locked the door. In those days, no one needed to tell Bob that this was a doom-laden omen foretelling a death. But whose death?

The answer wasn't long in coming. The following night cries for help were heard from the darkened road and, with his neighbours, Bob helped drag a fatally injured man from his overturned cart. A young man who didn't know the road had been driving the farmer and his wife home and had strayed off the track. Armstrong insisted that the light he had seen the previous evening had followed the precise path of the fated cart.

In Reformed Scotland, the connection between candles and the Roman Catholic Church may have something to do with such a sighting being regarded as a death omen. Although the use of candles for church ceremonies and decoration was discouraged by the Kirk, the practice continued right into the 1800s – a reflection, one suspects, of sentiments much deeper than mere religious dogma.

See also **Day of the Dead**

CELEBRITY

The problem with fame and a high-profile funeral is that every Tom, Dick and Willie would-be-wordsmith can have a go at eulogising the deceased. Alfred, Lord Tennyson got the treatment in 1892 from the Dundee bard William McGonagall. The introductory and concluding stanzas, as well as one from the body of the text will give an indication of the nature of the work:

Alas! England now mourns for her poet that's gone –
The late and good Lord Tennyson.
I hope his soul has fled to heaven above,
Where there is everlasting joy and love . . .

The bottom of the grave was thickly strewn with white roses,
And for such a grave kings will sigh where the poet now reposes;
And many of the wreaths were much observed and commented
   upon,
And conspicuous amongst them was one from Mrs Gladstone . . .

And, in conclusion, I most earnestly pray,
That the people will erect a monument for him without delay,
To commemorate the good work he has done,
And his name in gold letters written thereon!

CEMETERIES

Much of the credit for the austere Victorian way of death that is so obvious in the boneyards of Scotland's cities – and which lingers

43

even today – must go to a gentleman called John Claudius Loudon. He wrote extensively on the creation of ornamental gardens and the management of great country houses. For our purposes, he was also the man who penned the work that was largely responsible for the planning of cemeteries right into the twentieth century. It was entitled *On the Laying Out, Planting and Managing of Cemeteries and the Improvement of Churchyards* and was published in 1843.

Although it was the Victorian period, when we see the growth of cities of the dead to replace the crowded, insanitary old yards, a similar problem seems to have developed in the 1500s as towns such as Dundee and Edinburgh began to grow rapidly. Grants of land for new burying grounds – occasionally from royalty – can be traced in this period.

CHASING LIFE

So many metaphors have been used to explore the theme of death that it is sometimes difficult to sort out the most worthwhile. However, the poet William Drummond of Hawthornden, a product of the High School of Edinburgh, used a sporting theme to great effect in the first half of the seventeenth century:

> The World a Hunting is,
> The prey, poor Man,
> The Nimrod fierce is Death,
> His speedy Greyhounds are
> Lust, Sickness, Envy, Care,
> Strife that ne'er falls amiss,
> With all those ills which haunt us

While we breathe.
Now if (by chance) we fly
Of these the eager Chase,
Old Age with stealing Pace,
Casts up his Nets,
And there we panting die.

CHILDREN

Infant mortality was an all too common scourge in the Highlands of Scotland as well as in the crowded urban slums of the Central Belt. Little ones arrived and were gone in months, weeks or hours. As ever, there was a good old Scottish epitaph to match the sombre occasion:

> He that is born today and dies tomorrow,
> Loses hours of joys, but months of sorrow.

In areas like Lochaber, parents who had already lost children would name their newborn after the first person they met on their way to the kirk for the baptism. This was known popularly as giving the child a 'highway name'. Whether this is thought to have afforded some of protection to the child we can only wonder but there was always the danger that you might have ended up with a boy named Sue or, more likely, Mhorag.

Ernest Marwick, author of *The Folklore of Orkney and Shetland*, records that, in the Northern Isles, if a child died unbaptised, a note with their name was often pinned above their breast – a sort of passport to paradise.

CHIMNEY BOYS

What a nightmare! Into the dark, menacing vent, choked with soot, narrowing to as little as nine inches, the boy would squeeze himself. Pushing his brush in front of him, scrambling for a foothold on the steeper sections and twisting like an eel, he would use his knees and elbows to lever himself slowly, painfully forward into the Stygian gloom.

You would have thought that, for hundreds of climbing boys all across Scotland during the spring of 1842, the sun must have shone a little bit brighter and the air probably tasted that little bit sweeter. For, that summer, it became a criminal offence to compel a young person, under twenty-one years of age, to ascend or descend a chimney or enter a flue for the purpose of cleaning or coring it. And the legislation ordered that no one under sixteen should be apprenticed to the trade of chimney sweep.

The hope was that the 'rope and ball and other machinery' would take the place of the boy sweeps and that the few chimneys that were unsuitable for the use of these would be altered. Without a tabloid press around, it will disappoint you to learn that none of the journals carried the seemingly inevitable headline, 'Sweeping Changes Planned'.

But we digress. The new law, many felt, was long overdue. Boys were regularly trapped for hours inside chimney flues, wedged so tightly that masonry sometimes had to be knocked away to free them. Others, an unspecified but probably alarming number, suffocated in the sooty pipes, perhaps having cleaned up to thirty chimneys in a session.

Glasgow seems to have lagged behind other cities in locally out-lawing this 'disagreeable and laborious' occupation. *The Glasgow*

Herald had campaigned doggedly for a ban and, in an impassioned article written a couple of years before the 1842 legislation, the paper reported a horrible, claustrophobic death of a climbing boy. The piece declared:

> . . . we hope the day is not too distant when the plan of employing little creatures who should rather be in infant school than on the streets will be altogether disused.

The sweep-boys were usually barefoot and scantily clad and their shouts, around daybreak on bleak winter mornings, were one of the characteristic street sounds of mid-nineteenth-century Glasgow.

However, there was a problem with the new ban. Horrendous though this work might have been, it did provide employment and a few much-needed extra pennies to the family income. Smiles were not universal at news of the ban. And this legislation, which helped ease the cruel lot of thousands of kids, addressed only one dangerous aspect of using child labour. Around the same time as it came into force, a government report told of a nine-year-old boy 'trapper' working at Govan colliery. He opened and shut the ventilator doors and had to work twelve-hour shifts starting at 6 a.m. His entire day was spent sitting in a niche in the wall, without any light. For those working to bring the wee ones into the sunshine a lot of work remained to be done.

William Shakespeare used the chimney boys to stress death as the great equaliser. In two classic lines from *Cymbeline* he suggests:

> Golden lads and girls all must,
> As chimney-sweepers, come to dust.

CIVIL FUNERALS

Funerals without religious trappings took a while to reach Scotland. Humanist funerals, conducted by council registrars, are now available and it was South Lanarkshire Council that led the way in bringing funerals into line with civil marriages and baby-naming ceremonies. These non-traditional send-offs can include tributes from friends and relatives, readings of favourite poems or the playing of the deceased's favourite music. To date, they have been held in crematoriums. It is estimated that more than 1000 humanist-style funerals take place in Scotland annually and that this figure is rising.

CLOCKS

One of the most bizarre websites relating to death must be The Death Clock. It boasts of being the internet's quiet reminder that life is slipping away and is an American idea, of course. The idea is that you enter a few facts and figures about yourself – such as your weight, date of birth, etc. You then submit a few pieces of speculation – such as whether you think you are going to die of cancer, a stroke or by crashing your sports car on the way home from an all-night party at the age of ninety. Equipped with this info, The Death Clock will predict your death date.

As an old Orcadian pal was wont to say, 'This knowledge could be a good thing or it could be a bad thing.' However, if this is your idea of fun, then you'll find the clock ticking your life away at www.deathclock.com.

COFFINS

The word coffin comes from the Latin cophinus, meaning 'a basket or coffin'. We probably have the Egyptians to thank for the introduction of coffins – the only covering a Jewish corpse was given was its grave clothes. Graves of the Bronze Age often command an unobstructed view of the sea and an oak tree that had been split in two and hollowed out to form a coffin was found in 1850 on the north slope of the Castle Hill in Edinburgh.

A common coffin, normally called a bier, parish coffin or mort-kist by church authorities, was regularly used in Scotland to bury the poor in the sixteenth and seventeenth centuries. In 1602, the kirk session of Perth ordered 'ane common mort-kist, whereby the dead corpses of the poor ones may be honestly carried unto the burial'. Right into the nineteenth century, during the frequent famines and outbreaks of smallpox, cholera and plague that ravaged Scotland, a 'common coffin' was used to bury the poor with little dignity. These coffins were normally designed with hinged floors. As the coffin was being lowered into the ground, the floor would be opened, allowing the body to tumble into the grave so that the casket could be reused whenever necessary.

On the tombstone of Mr William M'Bean, merchant, Inverness, who died in 1694 is the inscription:

A coffin black is all we have
When we are laid into the grave

The truth is that many folk, especially in the Highlands, did not even have that. In Orkney, Shetland and the Hebrides, burial without coffins also seems to have been commonplace in centuries past. Anne

A linen press to be used as a coffin when the time is right (made by
The Scottish Vernacular Furniture Co., Cockburnspath)

Gordon says that, in Sutherland, a long basket of twisted rushes was sometimes used and it was known, rather quaintly, as a 'dead hamper'. It too would have been recovered once the deceased was safely in the grave.

From time to time, Americans wi' mair money than sense pay tribute to their legendary motor car industry by being buried in their favourite automobile. Little surprise then that, according to one estimate, American graveyards will be full by the year 2020.

COMBAT

In thirteenth-century Scotland, if trial by battle, in the form of a hand-to-hand duel, was arranged to settle a matter of honour, even dying did not excuse attendance. If, within a fortnight of the combat being arranged, someone died, the family were obliged to wheel the deceased along on the appointed day. It is thought this strange business protected the legal rights of the heirs. The corpse was usually put into the arena and had to be thrown or lifted over the surrounding barriers by the perplexed opponent before the matter could be declared closed, with honour satisfied.

COMFORTING THOUGHTS

† You can only die once
† Whom the Gods love die young
† The good die young

COMPASS

In large Scottish kirkyards, there was normally a geographical element that dictated who could be buried where. The north side of was traditionally reserved for suicides, murderers and often accident victims. The east was reserved for ecclesiastics. Members of the upper classes laid claim to the south side and the west ground was reserved for the rabblement.

COMPLEXION

In times past, if you encountered someone who looked like death warmed up, your reaction might have been to describe them as being 'like a wight oot o' anither world'.

COMPLIANCE

John, John, pit yer neck in the nic' tae please the lairdie!

According to Colin Walker, this bizarre saying stems from a supposed incident when a wife ordered her husband to stop resisting the laird's efforts to string him up. It has come to be applied to anyone who is too readily compliant with the orders of their boss.

COOLING

It is generally accepted that, under normal conditions, it takes the human body up to ten hours to cool after death. And rigor mortis, the stiffening of the joints and muscles after death, will usually be complete within twelve hours.

CORONACH

In societies all over the world, the chanting of dirges, often by women, is practised at funerals. In the Gaelic culture of Ireland and Scotland the name for this is the coronach. It has been variously described as a wailing lament and a hideous howl. However, listeners have also described it as haunting and plaintive. In the past, Highland communities often supported a 'professional' coronach singer. Again there are suggestions that the practice lasted into the twentieth century in some isolated corners of the Highlands.

In the 1700s, following the tragic, accidental death of two English soldiers at Kinlochcraig, the famous road-building General Wade thought it might be appropriate to employ hired mourners locally to 'keen' or formally mourn the dead in the traditional way. A group of MacMillan women were paid ten shillings for their professional services at the funeral. To a sad and mournful lament they sang the lines:

Ho, ro, hi, ho!
Dh fhalbh na sasunnaich,
Hi, hu, ho, hi!
S dar a tig an t-aon là thilleas iad.

This translates as:

Ho, ro, hi, ho!
The Sassenachs are gone,
Hi, hu, ho, hi!
And may the time ne'er come when they'll return.

General Wade, not having a grasp of the Gaelic, was said to be delighted with this splendidly ethnic tribute to his men.

CORPSE PRESENT

Among the tough dues which the medieval church exacted from Scots, none was more burdensome or more hated than the 'death due'. When a man died, the vicar of the parish was entitled to claim what was known as the 'corpse present' which was normally the deceased's best cow. In addition he also claimed the 'upmaist cloth' which fairly well explains itself. It was the deceased's uppermost bed covering.

These dues bore particularly heavily on the poorer folk and, in the Lowlands especially, were a cause of great suffering. When a small tenant died the vicar drove off the cow which he claimed, the superior of the land probably seized another and sometimes the Crown took a third while the 'upmaist cloth' could be exacted from almost any person, no matter how poverty stricken. In Inverness and presumably elsewhere in Scotland, by the late fifteenth century, the 'corpse present' and the 'upmaist cloth' were never again to be exacted from any free burgess of the burgh or his servants – a small cash payment was made for each child instead.

COSTS OF BURIAL

From the Parish of Logie just outside Stirling comes an interesting schedule of burial charges for 1872 and below are instructions for the gravedigger:

Category	Child Under 10	Adult
1 Paupers	–	3s 0d
2 Labourers	3s 0d	6s 0d
3 Middle Class	4s 6d	9s 0d
4 Upper Class and Visitors to Bridge of Allan (a popular spa)	6s 0d	12s 0d

As far as practicable, each grave was to be at least six feet deep. Fifty years earlier, during the bodysnatcher era, some graves on the outskirts of Edinburgh were dug to the depth of thirteen feet.

COVENANTERS

The Covenanter James White was brutally executed and beheaded and my nomination for Scotland's most graphic epitaph must go to the one on his headstone at Fenwick in Ayrshire. It reads:

This martyr was by Peter Inglis shot.
By birth a tigyr rather than a Scot,
Who that his monstrous extract might be seen,
Cut off his head & kick'd it o'er the green,
Thus was that head which was to wear a crown,
A football made by a profane dragoon.

CREMATION

Early Victorian cremationists had serious problems getting their message over. It was a court case in the 1880s, following elderly Dr

Covenanters' Memorial

William Price's attempt to cremate his five-month-old son, christened Jesus Christ, that brought the issue into the public arena. Price claimed to be a druid high priest and performed the ceremony in a white tunic. He was arrested and put on trial and it was as a result of this trial that, in 1884, cremation was declared legal.

The first crematorium was built the following year at Woking but it was the mid 1890s before Scotland had its first crematorium. At the last count, approximately seventy per cent of deaths that occur in the UK result in the deceased being cremated. This means that, annually, there are around 40,000 cremations in Scotland. However, cremation is still less popular in Scotland than elsewhere in the country. This is probably because of resistance to the practice from fundamentalist churches and Catholics of Irish descent.

> Mither: Alec . . .
> Faither: Aye, light o' my life?
> Mither: Alec, I think Ah'd like to be crematit.
> Faither: Right ye are then – get yer coat oan!
>
> (with thanks to Jerry Dennis)

Cremation was practised by our ancestors in Neolithic times but it was the overcrowded and unsanitary conditions in Victorian burial grounds which led to cremation being promoted as a hygienic and space-saving alternative. Its many advantages were soon appreciated.

The story is told of a couple who lived on the south side of Glasgow. Despite thirty years of marriage, they hated each other with a passion that was intense. After the old man died the dutiful wife visited the crematorium (which shall remain nameless) and asked in detail about the process of cremation from the moment the coffin slid through the curtains to the actual burning.

She was told that gas jets would provide an intense heat during the burning process and the widow nodded with satisfaction. As she examined the electrical machine for grinding the remaining bones into dust, the undertaker, who had also been asked to attend this briefing, thought he should take the opportunity to ask about the choice of music for the cremation service. Innocently, he inquired, 'What would you like to hear after the curtains close?'

The grieving widow thought for a moment and then responded icily, 'The scratching of nails from inside the coffin.'

> A: It's no good – I've got one foot in the grate.
> B: You mean grave?
> A: No, I mean 'grate' – I want to be cremated.
>
> (Max Kaufmann)

Connoisseurs of the bizarre and obscure agree that probably the most fetching opening line in modern Scottish literature is to be found in *The Crow Road* by Iain Banks – 'It was the day my grandmother exploded.' The explanation was that someone had forgotten to remove Granny's heart pacemaker before her cremation. This unlikely event is based on fact and I'm told that, despite strict regulations, such unwanted events still occur in Scotland.

Up there, alongside that classic, must be Alan Spence's opening stunner in *Way To Go* – 'I sat up in the coffin, reading a comic and eating a sherbet fountain.'

The cremation process, according to Caroline Quigley, is certainly not suitable for the squeamish or those of an age when they already feel the body disintegrating:

† Hair and skin are first to burn
† Muscles throughout the body contract
† The abdomen swells and splits
† Soft tissue is destroyed
† Bones are exposed
† The viscera disappear
† The bones glow
† The skeleton falls apart

Six to twelve pounds of ashes and bone fragments are produced in the normal cremation and, contrary to popular perception, individual cremation remains are kept separate throughout the process and not shovelled into an urn from a collective 'ash pan' at the end of a day's burning.

All Christian denominations including The Church of Scotland and the Roman Catholic Church permit cremation. The procedure is also acceptable to Sikhs, Buddhists and Hindus but is totally forbidden by Orthodox Jews and Muslims.

When the coffin drops out of sight or disappears discreetly behind the curtain in the crematorium, the last hymn has been sung and the mourners disperse, the work of the crematorium staff is really just beginning. In the crematory room, the nameplate is carefully checked to ensure the correct identity. An identity card accompanies the coffin and the cremated remains until their disposal or removal from the crematorium. It is possible for two family witnesses to see the coffin loaded into the cremator but the process itself is not open to inspection by the bereaved. Cremation authorities operate a national code of ethics, one specific injunction being that cremation is always completed on the same day as the service.

Currently, there are eighteen major crematoriums operating in

Scotland, principally in the east and central regions. The opening of Inverness crematorium meant that people from the Highlands and Islands no longer had to travel to Clydebank or Aberdeen for a cremation.

HOW CLOSE IS YOUR CREMATORIUM?

Aberdeen
Ayr
Buckie
Cardross
Clydebank
Dreghorn (Ayrshire)
Dundee
Dunfermline
Edinburgh: Leith
Edinburgh: Mortonhall
Edinburgh: Warriston
Glasgow: Craigton
Glasgow: Daldowie
Glasgow: The Linn
Glasgow: Maryhill
Inverness
Paisley
Perth

Dancing

Gae hop an' hang yourself',
Then you'll be dancin'.

I suspect this is not such a sinister injunction as it appears at first glance. Directed at someone who is getting on your nerves, the most reasonable proverbial simile which I can suggest is the old classic:

Away and raffle yersel' – that's the ticket!

In broadly the same category is the strange suggestion:

An' you get tae Hecklebirnie!

which is said to have been used as an injunction to someone who has told you to:

Get to the Devil!

The unholy parish of Hecklebirnie is, by tradition, located three miles beyond hell and would not be a comfortable place to spend eternity, I would guess.

Day of the Dead

Britain's National Day of the Dead falls in mid April each year. On the day, people visit woodland and other green burial sites. The event is run by a non-profit organisation called the Natural Death Centre and is based on the Mexican Day of the Dead, a fiesta of feasting and reunion and rekindling of connections with those who have gone before. Hallowe'en, coinciding with the Mexican festival, is the traditional British day of the dead but the Natural Death Centre has selected blushing springtime rather than gloomy autumn for their celebrations. The organisers encourage families to light a candle at mealtime and share memories of the dead. It may take a wee while to get this idea up and running, one suspects.

Deadlines

On her long trips to and from Balmoral, Queen Victoria, who detested speed, never allowed the royal train to travel at more than forty miles per hour. Ironically, her last rail journey, on board her funeral train through the south of England, was completed at speeds of up to 80 mph because it was running late.

Deadly Scottish Proverbs

† Efter a', whit's death? Just nature telling ye tae ca' canny
† Better be a coward than a corpse
† Fancy may kill or cure

† A man's o' little use when his wife's a widow
† Dead men are free men
† A' that ye'll tak wi' ye will be but a kist and a sheet, efter a'
† Dinna speak o' a rope tae a chiel whose faither was hangit
† Either live – or die – wi' honour
† Dead men dinnae bite
† Hang a thief when he's young and he'll no' steal when he's auld
† He gangs lang barefoot that waits for dead men's shoon
† Death and drink-draining are near neighbours
† When there's death at ae door, there's hardship at the other
† He that wears black maun wear a brush on his back
† Death comes and spears nae questions
† If you wad live forever, wash the milk from your liver
† I'll kiss ye when ye're sleeping and that'll hinder ye to dream of me when you're deid
† Death has no favourites
† He that's born to be hanged will ne'er be drowned
† Death defies the doctor
† Death settles a' scores

DEALING WITH DEATH

In the funeral trade in Scotland, it is generally recognised that Roman Catholics tend to cope with bereavement better than their Presbyterian counterparts. The explanation is that it is probably a mystical 'Celtic' thing. The whole bedrock of the Catholic faith is that death is not the end. There is certainly sorrow at the loss but this is matched with joy and celebration in the knowledge that the person has gone to a better place. In the experience of the funeral trade, the more rational view of the Protestant faith does not appear to offer the same comfort.

Another group who appear to have problems coming to terms with death is the well-off. There always seems to be greater degree of involvement and self-reliance among ordinary people when it comes to handling death and the further up the affluence ladder you climb into the middle classes, the more difficulty people seem to have. They will do everything to avoid having the funeral from the house. The manifestation of mourning is frowned on by this group and, if they can get away with it, their funerals are generally fairly private. A vulnerability, a lack of control, is exposed in these successful people at the critical moment when there is a death in the family.

DEATH

† Is a great leveller
† Pays all Debts

DEATH AND THE ENGLISH

The image of our English cousins in the face of eternity is a formidable one. True grit was displayed everywhere they went throughout the great Empire. But they have been characterised over the centuries by the need to remain unflustered when confronted with the greatest of life's troubles up to, and including, death. The novelist Pamela Frankau skilfully summarised this perceived sangfroid of the English:

The English find ill-health not only interesting but respectable and often experience death in the effort to avoid a fuss.

However, given the displays – some would say the excessive displays – of grief that were shown on the death of Diana, Princess of Wales, this is perhaps not quite so true as it used to be.

DEBT

A working group of Parliamentarians is currently examining debt in Scotland and one issue under scrutiny is the spiralling cost of funerals. A recent survey by the *Daily Record* discovered that the costs for a coffin, a parlour viewing, one hearse, one car for mourners and simple cremation could range from around £600 to as much as £2000. More and more people are getting into financial difficulties by trying to give their loved ones the kind of send-off they feel they deserve.

DECORATION

In 1857 in Wester Anstruther, Fife, in a room ornamented with shells, a man who worked as slater and plasterer exhibited his coffin. It was covered with seashells and painted black. Eccentric, aye just a bittie!

DEFYING DEATH

An intriguing advert appeared in the Scottish press in July 1879, when a representative of that timeless breed, the quack healers, offered 'The Magneticon – The Great Curative Agent' which he claimed would cure paralysis and general debility. One testimonial for the appliance read:

> Through being struck by lightning my wife's health was prostrated and her nervous system completely shattered. I purchased for her the Magneticon and since then she has become a real livewire.

Right enough!

DELAYS

It's said that Satan was up to all sorts of tricks to prevent clergymen reaching the dying to offer them comfort at the end of their lives. As recently as the mid nineteenth century, a minister at Glenmoriston in the Loch Ness district was making his way to the house of a dying man when he heard the sound of a baby crying by the roadside. He picked up the child, which was wrapped in a shawl, and decided to take the little bundle with him. However, as he trekked onwards the child grew heavier and heavier until he had to rest. At this point, the baby turned into a hideous monster with horrible, horny fingers which seized the minister by the throat. By invoking the name of God, the minister made the satanic beast disappear in a flash of light and was then able to hurry on and bring peace to the dying man. Mind you, after that encounter you kind of suspect he would be in need of a wee bit comfort himself!

Walter, First Earl of Buccleuch, was finally buried at Hawick in 1634 months after the ship carrying his body north from England was blown to Norway in a storm.

The creator of Sherlock Holmes, Edinburgh-educated Sir Arthur Conan Doyle, was an enthusiastic spiritualist in his later life and regularly had a blether with the residents of the far side. So confident was he of the reality of the afterlife that, on one occasion when warned that a friend was dying and that tomorrow might be too late to visit, Conan Doyle chirpily responded, 'In that case, I'll speak to him next week.'

DESTINY

There's nae fleeing fae Fate.

DEVIOUSNESS IN DEATH

Evan Dhu Maccombish, a character in Sir Walter Scott's *Waverley*, displays the loyalty and fearlessness in the face of death traditionally associated with the Scottish Highlander. Having watched his chieftain Fergus MacIvor sentenced to death for his part in the Forty-Five uprising, Evan boldly asks to be allowed to speak and suggests to the astonished court that, if the judge will set MacIvor free, six of the clan would willingly offer themselves up to 'head or hang' in his place 'and you may begin wi' me the very first man'. His offer is met by laughter in court. An infuriated Evan, scolding the 'Saxon gentlemen', says that, if they are amused because they do not believe he will keep his word, 'I can tell them they ken neither the heart of a Highlandman nor the honour of a gentleman.'

But we must add another, perhaps more subtle, element to this kind of legendary bold, occasionally reckless, behaviour in the face of death. The red 'Celtic mist' has its counterpart in deviousness – ingenuity that still has the power to make us gasp in admiration.

This is well illustrated by a remarkable incident concerning the Scottish presence in North America during the French and Indian wars of the mid-eighteenth century. In January 1757, officers of the newly formed Montgomery's Highlanders were commissioned and the Scots soldiers set off almost immediately for Canada. In the wild country south of the Great Lakes, they were used in small, mobile groups, ranging across the vast forested landscape and engaging in a series of skirmishes with their French enemies who were supported by Indian allies.

Inevitably, some of the Highlanders fell into hands of the Indians, whose bloodthirsty techniques of torture were whispered around the military stockades. One of the prisoners, Allan Macpherson, was forced to watch the miserable, protracted agonies of his comrades before they died under torture. Realising that his turn had come, Macpherson made urgent signs indicating that he had something of importance to communicate. In his book, *Sketches of the Highlanders in Scotland*, Colonel David Stewart explains how Macpherson told the Indians that, providing his life was spared for a few minutes, he would pass on the secret of an extraordinary ointment which, if applied to the skin, would harden it against the strongest blow of a tomahawk or sword. All he asked was to be allowed to go into the woods, under guard, to collect plants needed for this medicine. He would prepare it and offer his neck to the strongest and most expert warrior to test its efficacy. The astonished Native Americans agreed to the request, despite the possibility that it might be the cover for some clever escape plan.

Macpherson returned with the berries and plants, doctored them up with elaborate precision and then rubbed his neck with the juice.

Laying his head upon the log, he asked the chosen warrior to strike his mightiest blow, saying he did not expect to sustain the merest scratch. The Indian struck hard and true and with such force that Macpherson's head flew off for a distance of several yards.

After a moment or two of stunned silence, the Indians realised that they had been duped in the most cunning manner and, stunned by the skill with which the prisoner had avoided a lingering death, they abandoned plans to torture the remainder of the captives. Among the lodges for decades afterwards, the deviousness in death of the Scot Allan Macpherson was spoken of with wonder and admiration.

DISCOVERIES

The exact location of the grave of Scotland's patriot king, Robert Bruce, had long been forgotten. But, in February 1818, workmen at Dunfermline Abbey discovered his bones. Robert the Bruce had been among the first kings of Scotland to be buried at Dunfermline and, when his bones were reinterred below the pulpit of the rebuilt church in 1819, he also became the last.

There was a ghoulish sensation in May 1795 when the body of Lady Dundee and her infant child were found in a state of perfect preservation in the Viscounts of Kilsyth's vault in Kilsyth Church. She and the child had been killed in a building collapse in Rotterdam more than a century before and, after embalming, the bodies had been transported to Scotland for burial. Some hooligans forced their way into the vault, tore up a lead coffin and found a fresh one of fir inside, enclosing the two bodies, 'looking as fresh as if they were only asleep'. According to the reports:

The shroud was clean, the ribbons of the dress unruffled, not a fold or knot discomposed. The child, plump, and with the smile of innocence arrested on its lips, excited pity and admiration in every beholder. A patch on the lady's forehead concealed the wound which had caused her death. When the face was uncovered, beautiful auburn hair and a fine complexion, with a few pearly drops like dew upon her face, occasioned in the crowd of onlookers a sigh of silent wonder.

The woman's husband, Viscount Kilsyth, had forfeited his title and estate in the 1715 uprising so there was no descendant to 'enforce respect' for the remains. It was, therefore, left to a local gentleman to ensure that the coffin and vault were properly sealed again. This was done only after 'public curiosity' had been satisfied. As to the fate of the grave wreckers, there is no word.

DO-IT-YOURSELF FUNERALS

Surprisingly, perhaps, it appears that, under UK law as it stands – provided mains and drain services are not interfered with and no profit is made – a body can be buried more or less anywhere. You can even pick up your loved one in your own vehicle and bury them in your own back yard. A warning comes, however, from the Natural Death Centre in London about that homely disposal – garden burials, not surprisingly, can devalue a property by between 20 and 50 per cent.

DOCTORS

Raising or restoring the apparently dead in the mid sixteenth century could become something of a theatrical performance if the strange tale of Robert Henderson is anything to go by. In the summer of 1563, he had attracted the favourable notice of the town council of Edinburgh by performing 'sundry wonderful cures'.

If we are to believe the chroniclers, his medical achievements were quite remarkable. They included:

† 'healing' a man whose hands had been cut off;
† restoring a man and a woman, who had been run through the body with swords, to health;
† and, most impressively, bringing a woman, who was understood to have suffocated and who had 'lain two days in her grave', back to life.

The council awarded Robert thirty merks for this work. It was clearly cheap at the price.

The power of 'doctors' over the patients in life-or-death situations is immense. Sir Walter Scott tells of being in an English county town when one of his servants took unwell and the local doctor was called in. Imagine Scott's amazement when he came face to face with a blacksmith/vet from the Borders who had disappeared some time before. The man had re-emerged after all those years as a well-respected physician.

When they were alone Scott, worried about this clandestine change of calling, asked, 'But, John, do you never happen to kill any of your patients?'

The 'doctor' explained that sometimes they died and sometimes they didn't, adding, 'Onyhow, Maister Scott, it will be lang before it maks up for Flodden!'

DOORSTEP DEATH

The saga of the Forty-Five has more romantic tragedy woven into its bloody fabric than perhaps any other episode in Scottish history. The victory by the Jacobite army over the government forces under Sir John Cope at Prestonpans near Edinburgh could be seen as the campaign high point for Bonnie Prince Charlie's Highland army.

My own favourite bittersweet tale of the rebellion centres on this battle but paradoxically it involves the fate of a senior officer on the government side – Colonel James Gardiner. He was born at Carriden in what was Linlithgowshire and, at the age of fourteen, obtained a commission in a Scots regiment in the Dutch service. He moved to the English army and fought at Blenheim before being badly wounded in 1706 at Ramillies. By 1715 he was a captain of dragoons and with eleven others, eight of whom were killed, was responsible for setting fire to the Highlanders' barricades at Preston during the Jacobite uprising of that year.

By the time of Prestonpans, Gardiner was in his fifty-eighth year and a colonel. He found himself fighting his final battle within sight of his home, Bankton House, a mansion, now renovated, lying to the south of the present-day Prestonpans railway station.

This battle became notorious for the bloodthirstiness of the clansmen and has been used to excuse the violent reaction of government forces at Culloden. The Highlanders, wielding scythes lashed to long poles, waded into the government ranks slashing at the horses' noses and scattering Gardiner's dragoons within minutes.

Col. Gardiner's Monument, with his home, Bankton house, in the background

Harvest at Inveraray

The colonel put himself in charge of the hard-pressed foot soldiers as they were pushed back towards the high walls of Bankton House. Even as he encouraged his men in the face of the Highland onslaught, he was felled by a terrible blow from a Lochaber axe, a particularly vicious hooked cutting weapon, and was finished off as he tumbled to the ground.

Having fought all over Britain and Europe, he died in a pitched battle a few yards from his own front door. Perhaps mercifully, he was spared the sight of the ensuing slaughter that took place against the walls of the mansion, as the infantrymen, having discarded their weapons, were herded together and cut to pieces with sword and axe.

DOPPELGANGERS

It was a common belief in rural Scotland of centuries past that an exact image of the dying person might appear in his or her most familiar surroundings around or at the time of death. Another strange Scandinavian belief referred to by Ernest Marwick was that a 'varden' or companion spirit accompanied a person throughout their life and set up a mournful wailing at the time of death. The 'varden' was often in the shape of an animal.

DREAMS

One of the strangest aspects of the interpretation of dreams is the fact that to dream of death is generally accepted as a very positive sign, often indicating a wedding or a birth in the family. Paradoxically to dream of a birth may be a sign of an impending death. Confused? Me too! Here are a few other death-significant dreams:

† To dream of an owl (for all you twitchers, the variety is not specified) indicates a narrow escape from death
† To dream of the loss of teeth or of fingers was regarded among the early mining communities in Fife as sign of impending death
† To dream of a ship sailing across the land was regarded in many areas, for example in the Northern Isles, as a sure indicator of death. Occasionally, so tradition has it, people with sons at sea who had such a strange dream would shortly thereafter learn of their death
† To dream of riding a bike downhill at speed, unsurprisingly, is regarded as a death omen
† To dream of crows, as you might expect, is said to be an indication of major impending grief
† To dream of a deceased person is not a cause for alarm. The dreamer should listen very carefully to what the dead person has to say – it could help shape the rest of their life
† To dream of marriage or a wedding dream indicates a death in the family
† To dream of a necklace suggests the death of a loved one
† To dream of a barking dog foretells sorrow (or someone trying to climb through your kitchen windae!)

And there are dozens of other such interpretations. The fact that to dream of a well-kept cemetery suggests future happiness sounds to me, with apologies to Dr Freud, as though we shouldn't get too hung up on the meaning of dreams.

DRINK

There's Death in the cup – so beware!

'Inscription on a Goblet'
Robert Burns (1759–96)

An interesting debate was raging in the columns of *The Glasgow Herald* in January 1876 over the revelation that Marwood, the public executioner, was not a teetotaller. When he was on 'offishell' business at Dumbarton, he had apparently, over a period of three or four days, consumed one bottle of brandy, one bottle of whisky and one dozen of bitter beer. The town council were refusing to pay the bill, accusing him of extravagance. *The Herald* felt that, in providing the 'necessary but not nice' service as hangman, he might require a little more stimulant for his duties than the councillors might consider suitable.

It seems that no self-respecting funeral was complete without copious quantities of drink being taken. A sober commentator observed, 'Too often the unlimited use of stimulants turned their grief to merriment.' An Act of the General Assembly in 1695 ordered an elder or deacon to be present at all coffinings. Their job was a very simple one – to keep order. Great crowds are reported at aristocratic funerals and generally more alcohol was consumed and more tobacco taken than at weddings.

Sydney, Australia, was the location of one of the most insensitive police actions in the nation's history. A squad of police officers pulled over a funeral procession and made all the drivers, including a priest, take a breath test.

DUELLING

Death by duelling is legal in the South American country of Paraguay. There is one proviso – the event can only take place if both duellers are registered blood donors.

When duelling was at its peak in France between 1589 and 1607, it's said that over 4,000 noblemen were fatally ventilated in duels, an average of more than one every two days.

Scotland's most famous arena of duelling was below Arthur's Seat in Edinburgh.

Easy Life

Death has got something to be said for it:
There's no need to get out of bed for it;
Wherever you may be,
They bring it to you, free.

'Delivery Guaranteed'
Kingsley Amis

Efficiency

Try that for Size, Deacon

The trapdoor drop used to improve the efficiency of hanging was introduced and improved in Edinburgh by the notorious Deacon Brodie, master joiner, town councillor and man of mystery. When his double life as a housebreaker was exposed, he was sentenced to death and, in October 1783, he was among the first to test the effectiveness of his invention. Previously the condemned person had been pushed from a high platform but Brodie developed a trapdoor and lever system which became the industry standard. On the gallows, Deacon Brodie was bizarrely called upon to inspect the arrangements. He pronounced them satisfactory and then stepped on to his platform and into eternity. Bizarre!

ENIGMATIC SAYINGS

We are a' life-like – and daith-like.

Traditional Scottish saying

Who was it that said the living are the dead on holiday?

Terry Nation

If you don't go to other people's funerals they won't come to yours.

Anon.

ENTHUSIASM

In Arbroath in 1732, gravediggers were enthusiastically working on Sundays much to the displeasure of the kirk session who ordered a halt to this unusual – but some would say very necessary – form of Sabbath-breaking.

EPITAPHS (NOBLE AND OTHERWISE)

One of the best, he's now at rest.

Death's a thing inevitable,
It spares no rank or age,
The Old, the Young, the Rich, the Poor,
It doth pull off the stage.

Remember man as thow goes by,
As thow art now so once was I.
As I am now so most thow be,
Remember man that thow most di.

Found on the gravestone of James Kai (d. 1682) at St Andrews, the last of the above epitaphs was one of the most popular, if cheerless, sentiments displayed on Scottish gravestones from the seventeenth century onwards. And, occasionally, a Victorian version is encountered with a final line that runs:

Prepare for death and follow me.

In his book *The Undertaking*, Thomas Lynch refers to a creative individual who coined a neat response to this rather sombre sentiment:

To follow you I won't consent,
Until I know which way you went.

The Rev. John Pinkerton's epitaph from his gravestone at Markinch in Fife is a masterpiece of terse reportage:

After having spent a
Very cheerfull evening at
Balfour House with Mr
Bethune and his Family
He was found in the Morning
In his Bedroom sitting in
A chair by the Fireplace
with one stocking in his hand
quite dead.

My own favourite Scottish epitaphs, from both the genuine and the perhaps apocryphal, include the following:

Here lies interred a man o' micht,
His name was Malcolm Downie,
He lost his life ae market nicht,
By fa'n aff his pownie.

(Aberdeen)

Erected to the memory of John Macfarlane
Drowned in the Water of Leith,
By a few affectionate friends.

(Leith)

Here snug in Grave my wife doth lie,
Now she's at Rest – And so am I!

(Edinburgh)

And just to show that beyond the Border they could occasionally come up with a wee belter:

Here Lies John Yeast –
Forgive Him for Not Rising.

One of the most famous of Robbie Burns's creations was Holy Willie, the hypocritical kirk elder. But, in Willie's epitaph, Burns suggests that the old bugger got his predictable comeuppance:

Here Holy Willie's sair worn clay,
Taks up its last abode;
His soul has ta'en some other way,
I fear, the left-hand* road.

* to Hell!

And for the connoisseur of immortality a snippet from those masters of mirth Eric Morecambe and Ernie Wise:

Ernie: What would you like them to put on your tombstone?
Eric: Something short and simple
Ernie: What?
Eric: Back in five minutes!
Eddie Braben, *The Best of Morecambe and Wise*, 1974

In the same vein, that jolly chappie W C Fields, when asked to suggest an epitaph for himself, offered, 'I'd rather be living in Philadelphia.'

ERRORS

Robert Henderson, in his book *Scottish Keeriosities*, collected a whole series of misspellings and other errors from Scottish gravestones. He cites, for example, the remarkable death of Isabella Gilmour at Sanquhar, Dumfriess-shire, which took place, or so it seems, on 'April 31, 1862'.

EUPHEMISMS

Euphemisms for the words and phrases connected with death abound – there are probably more euphemisms connected to death than any other subject you can think of. It's not really surprising that people want to avoid direct mention of this taboo subject but this urge to make the reality of death less stark also has its darker side and sometimes the replacements are far grimmer than the original words. Here is a far-from-definitive list:

FOR DEATH
The Great Leveller
Old Man Mose
The Grim Reaper
The End of the Road
The Grim Monarch
The End of the Road

FOR DYING
Give up the ghost
Pass over
Meet your maker

Kick the bucket
Cash in your chips
Call it a day
Hand in your dinner plate
Croak it
Take an early bath
Lay down your knife and fork
Go down for the long count
Breathe your last
Shuffle off the mortal coil
Go belly, or toes, up
Jack it in
Be blotted off the map
Sing your swansong
Snuff it
Take the final curtain

FOR THE CORPSE

The deceased
Food for worms
The loved one
The silent passenger
Fly bait
Dog meat
Crow bait
Stiff
Stinker
Floater

FOR THE FUNERAL
Salted away
Sewn up in a blanket
Put on ice
Put six feet under
Put to bed with a shovel
Gone for a dirt nap
Off to a bed of clay

EXCARNATION

excarnation *noun* the act of depriving, clearing or divesting of flesh

This is one dictionary's definition of the word but it also refers to the practice of leaving the dead out in the open, exposed to the elements – in other words until the bones had been blasted by the elements and picked clean by the creepy and feathered ones. The ancient Celts, some Native Americans and certain other cultures were fans of this method of waste body disposal – I guess it must have been a bit like living amongst the seagulls of Aberdeen before the wheelie bins were introduced.

On my home island of Papa Westray there is a group of mysterious stone piles on the North Hill bird sanctuary. On investigation, these were found to contain 'cramp' or remnants of burnt human bone. The Hewitson theory is that the Neolithic dead of Papay were left out to be pecked at by the clouds of birds usually found on the hill, then the bones were burned and crushed and placed in urns before being carried across to the Holm of Papa

Westray. This mysterious little island shows no signs of ever having been settled but was clearly an important sacred site, having three tombs including an impressive chambered tomb at the south end of the isle. Within the tomb there is a cluster of what I would call family, or clan, chambers – the last resting place of the ancient dead of Papa Westray.

EXCAVATION

These days, gravediggers are required to know how to operate complex digging equipment rather than simply how to swing a shovel or a pickaxe. However, even into the twentieth century, the excavation of graves in difficult locations often required dynamite. Dynamite sheds still feature in some Scottish graveyards. The skills, strength and bravery that Irish labourers used on the canals and railway networks of Scotland were also frequently called for in this unusual work.

EXCUSES

In Scotland, it seems we work very hard on the excuses for not getting involved in a discussion of the Big D (yet another euphemism) and it's clear that we're in denial about lifestyles with possibly fatal consequences. Here are some of the most common excuses and denials encountered when people are unwilling or can't afford the time to talk about death:

† I don't drive all that fast!

† My grandfather lived till he was ninety
† This is too heavy a subject for a sunny day
† I'm too young to discuss that
† Nae worries – I've plenty of life insurance
† I'm a spiritualist – death's a doddle
† I can't afford the time to think about it
† I'm immortal
† Five black puddin' suppers a week – that's nothing
† You see enough o' it on the telly

EXECUTIONS

Alexander Cockburn, an Edinburgh public executioner, was himself sentenced to death in 1692 for murdering a beggar in his house.

Gruesome public executions were still one of the entertainment highlights for countless thousands of Scots in the early nineteenth century when the nation was steadily becoming industrialised and, according to the optimists, more civilised.

In late January 1815, *The Glasgow Herald* recorded the execution of two highway robbers in Edinburgh:

> They were escorted along Lawnmarket, West Bow, Grassmarket, and Wester Portsburgh, by the magistrates, high constables, and city guard. The magistrates delivered the prisoners to the sheriffs of the county, and they were escorted by sheriff officers and policemen to the place of execution.
>
> After conversing with two Catholic clergymen, they ascended the fatal drop, and about three o'clock were launched into eternity. Their conduct became their awful situation; and their dreadful

example will, it is hoped, repress those scenes of outrage with which the country has of late been disgraced.

A vast concourse of spectators assembled in Lawnmarket, Grassmarket, and other streets through which the procession passed. An immense crowd went to the place of execution; and the road and fields being covered with snow, they had the appearance of a solid, black column moving along the road. Notwithstanding the number of people not the smallest accident happened.

Across in Glasgow, around the same time, the position of public executioner was causing some anxiety to the city council. They were looking for a hangman, the previous incumbent apparently having brought a 'degree of disgrace' to the post. Councillors were seeking a 'well-behaved, sober man'.

The execution of Covenanter David Hackston of Rathillet at the Cross in Edinburgh 1680 is generally accepted as the most barbaric of a particularly bloody period in Scottish history. However, one macabre aspect of this event is seldom recalled. First of all, before being strung up, Hackston was to have his hands severed but the hangman bungled the first cut to the right hand and was then advised by Hackston himself how to make a more efficient job of the left hand.

Contempt for authority was something treated very seriously in centuries past. In particular, you did not deliberately or inadvertently insult or question the sanity of the monarch. Dire consequences could ensue. This was particularly true during the bloody years of the Covenanter Wars. In 1681, a huge crowd gathered in the Grassmarket, Edinburgh's traditional place of execution, to watch the despatch of three men who had, so we're told, questioned the king's authority. At the last moment, before the nooses were slipped around their necks, the trio were told that, if they were prepared to say 'God Save the King!', they would be spared. They refused.

A similar offer was made during one of Scotland's most notorious executions four years later when two female Covenanters were put to death by drowning, tied to stakes in a narrow channel at Bladenoch, a mile from Wigtown. It's said that Margaret MacLauchlan and Margaret Wilson steadfastly refused to say 'God Save the King!'.

Failure to declare loyalty to the Crown resulted in the completion of other executions around this trying time.

It was widely believed that death by guillotine was the swiftest and most sure way of instant oblivion – others, with good reason it seems, just weren't so sure this was true. One French executioner arranged for a condemned friend to signal him after being guillotined and, according to Christine Quigley, after the blade dropped the executioner was rewarded with a wink from the severed head. Hairs on the back of my neck stood on end when I also discovered that other tests have shown that a detached head may remain conscious for up to thirty seconds.

Mary Queen of Scots' lips are said to have continued to move for up to fifteen minutes after she was beheaded at Fotheringay Castle. And definitely in the 'Aye, right!' category is the story of Sir Everard Digby who was executed for complicity in the Gunpowder Plot to blow up James VI & I. The axeman, having severed Everard's napper from his body, removed his heart, exhibited it to the people and made the customary declamation, 'Here is the heart of a traitor.' At this point, according to the chroniclers, his severed head is said to have declared, quite distinctly, to the people nearest the block, 'Thou liest!'

Appointed in 1814, Glasgow's last professional executioner was Thomas Young. He helped seventy criminals to step into eternity and was driven to his sinister work in a coach after a slap-up meal washed down with brandy and claret. Hangmen in Scotland in centuries past usually received payment in kind and this could take many bewildering forms – for instance, in Aberdeen, he was entitled to a fish from every fishwife's creel.

Someone whose lifestyle might lead them into serious trouble, and possibly a date with the public executioner, might be warned in centuries past, particularly in Edinburgh, 'You'll gang up the Lawnmarket yet!'

Twenty-year-old Black Watch private John Docherty was executed on the Western Front for desertion, becoming the first Kitchener volunteer to be shot.

A Wee Tune Afore Ye Go

Perhaps the most bizarre execution seen in Scotland was that of the freebooter James McPherson at Banff in 1700. The victim, a great exponent of the fiddle, was allowed to play up until his final moments. He then smashed the instrument over his knee when no one volunteered to adopt it. It is also said that the town clock was advanced to forestall any chance of a reprieve. Our national bard was sufficiently moved by McPherson's bravery to reflect:

> Now farewell, light, thou sunshine bright',
> And all beneath the sky!
> May coward shame distain his name,
> The wretch that dares not die!

'McPherson's Farewell'
Robert Burns (1759–96)

91

VERY NECESSARY ANONYMITY

The traditional black mask of the hangman or executioner meant that the perpetrator of bungled executions could not be identified and suffer the wrath of the mob thereafter. In 1840, it is on record that a hangman at a Scottish execution withdrew the wrong bolt and the poor soul was left waiting for a wee eternity with the noose around his neck. To hisses and groans from the crowd an officer ran forward to the scaffold and released the correct bolt.

FACING THE AXE

Bold Balmerino is not one of the first Jacobite figures to spring to mind when talk turns to the Forty-Five uprising. The man went to meet his maker beneath the executioner's axe on Tower Hill in the summer of 1746. However, it was in his last moments that he was confirmed as a hero to his fellow Jacobites with such a positive performance on the scaffold that he left his executioners stunned. The Scots nobleman graciously but bizarrely spent most of his time trying to make others round about him feel at ease – so much so that he had eventually to apologise to the crowd for his apparent devil-may-care attitude on the edge of eternity.

The first significant mention of Arthur Elphinstone, Sixth Lord Balmerino, comes with the Jacobite uprising of 1715 when, on the accession of George I, he resigned his commission and was with the Earl of Mar at the indecisive action at Sheriffmuir, between Perth and Stirling. Arthur fled to France to begin an exile which was to last twenty years. However, due to some powerful lobbying by his faither, the British government granted him a free pardon and, with the Pretender's blessing (and some useful Jacobite pocket money), he returned to Scotland. With this pedigree, it's no surprise at all to learn that Balmerino was one of the first to join Bonnie Prince Charlie when he raised his standard at Glenfinnan at the start of the Forty-Five. He was appointed Colonel and had charge of the second troop of horse lifeguards attending the prince. He was at Carlisle when the town surrendered and in the famous Highland column which penetrated as far as Derby.

Taken prisoner by Cumberland's forces after Culloden, he was transported to London. Proceedings were simple and straightforward. Witnesses were examined who confirmed he had been with the 'rebels' at several locations during the campaign and he was sentenced to death along with Lord Kilmarnock and the Earl of Cromartie (who was later pardoned).

On the appointed day and immediately following the execution of Kilmarnock, Lord Balmerino was led to the scaffold and astonished onlookers by springing up the steps, striding round the platform and stooping to read the inscription on his coffin:

Arturus Dominus de Balmerino, decollatus 18vo die Augusti 1746, aetatis 58

He indicated his approval and then, when the executioner begged forgiveness, Balmerino halted him in mid sentence, saying, 'Friend, you need not ask me forgiveness. The execution of your duty is commendable.' He then bunged the axe-man three guineas, apologised for not having more money and bequeathed him his coat and waistcoat.

It was at this point that Balmerino realised folk might have found him a trace too cool, bearing in mind he faced imminent execution, and he turned to a gentleman nearby, declaring, 'I'm afraid there are some who may think my behaviour bold. Remember, sir, what I tell you, it arises from a confidence in God, and a clear conscience.' Then, taking the axe from the executioner, he felt its edge and returned it to him, showing where to strike the blow and urging him to 'do it with resolution for in that, friend, will consist your mercy'. The deed done, he was buried along with the Earl of Kilmarnock in the chapel of the Tower of London and, as he had no children, the male line of this branch of the Elphinstone family died with him.

FAITH

The very first mention of a Scot in Canada comes in the writings of the French explorer Samuel de Champlain who, in the early 1600s, tells of an unnamed Scots Huguenot in his party who died during a particularly severe winter. Even on his deathbed and after a lifetime with his Catholic comrades, the Scot rejected the opportunity to convert to Roman Catholicism.

FASTING

John Scott, the 'Teviotdale Faster', was a religious fanatic of the mid sixteenth century. He was said to have performed several amazing fasts both in the British Isles and on the Continent. Paradoxically, fasting became his meal ticket. The people of Venice had been particularly stunned by his lengthy public fast but, after setting up his own temple at the West Port in Edinburgh, he was hounded out of business as a crank and died, ironically but maybe not surprisingly, from overeating.

While the defeated Scots Covenanting army at the Battle of Dunbar in 1650 had been following the kirk's orders and fasting for days before the clash, Cromwell's victorious English 'croppies' had thrived on a diet consisting mainly of haggis by the ton. Now there's an ironic twist, is it not? The result is a pretty spectacular vote in favour of a haggis diet – over 3,000 Covenanters were killed and Cromwell counted his losses at forty.

FATAL LAST WORDS

General George Armstrong Custer, who is said by some genealogists to be descended from the Orcadian Cursiters (although he is also claimed by Germany), rode his luck as well as his horse throughout the Civil War. In fact, at least a dozen horses are said to have been shot from under him during the conflict. However, while fighting the Sioux, his good fortune famously deserted him at the Battle of the Little Big Horn. A supremely confident individual, his last comment, which surely confirms his Scottishness, was reported to be, 'Weel, lads, we hae them noo – let's get in among thae reed deevels and get hame fur oor tea!' A famous Indian victory followed.

FEAR OF DEATH

One of the worthies of nineteenth-century Errol, a big man called Peter Reid, earned a shilling on one occasion by wading chest deep into the River Tay at Port Allen to retrieve the body of a drowned man. As officials puzzled over a mode of transport for the deceased, Peter slung the corpse over his shoulder and marched off in the direction of Errol. Asked if he had not been afraid while retrieving the body, he vowed he would 'gang in for anither man themorrow.' It is worthwhile asking why the deep-seated fear of death is so widespread in Western society when it seems to be better handled in the so-called developing countries. Here are some possible reasons:

1. The decline in formal religious practice in Western nations has limited belief in the afterlife, rebirth and the concepts of heaven – and hell.
2. Family and community structures are disintegrating in the West and support systems for the bereaved are often inadequate.
3. We all watch far too many scary movies with chainsaws, face masks, extra-long metal fingernails and hands that reach out to pull you kicking and screaming into the underworld.
4. Children who grow up in this crazy world of death and destruction, whether make-believe or news generated, are, at the same time, shielded and insulated from the reality of death in the family setting.
5. Whereas in developing countries people generally still die at home, this is not the case in the developed nations where hospital death is the norm.
6. Mortality rates are far higher in the population of developing countries for infants, children and adults alike and, therefore, death, though unwelcome as ever, is a regular and familiar visitor.

FEUDING

Inter-clan disputes were a part of Scottish life for a thousand years. Less well-known are the bitter feuds between localities which could endure almost as long. Strangely, funerals were often seen as a suitable occasion for sorting out longstanding grievances.

One of the most enduring and intense feuds was between the Glenelg and Lochalsh districts in the Northwest and it was the funeral of Mrs Flora Macdonnell, at Glenelg in December 1814, when the rivalry spilled over into mob violence. After the funeral and a meal the party of men from Lochalsh returned to their boat but en route a dispute arose with a Glenelg resident who followed them to the shore. One of the Lochalsh men brought the debate to a conclusion by ducking the other man in the sea. The victim in turn called for help and the entire Lochalsh party, by then on board their boat, were set upon by a group of men 'armed with bludgeons' who had answered the call and proceeded to knock seven shades of sharn out of everyone on the boat.

Most of the Lochalsh team suffered serious cuts and bruises and there was, apparently, 'much effusion of blood'. The boat only escaped when someone cut a rope and it drifted into deeper water. Thereupon, the Glenelg gang showered the boat with stones as it departed.

For all the wrong reasons the day of Flora Macdonnell's funeral was long remembered in the two communities.

Even more serious was an incident in the Great Glen in the previous century with the funeral of an old woman. The Glenmoriston men wanted to take her west for burial; the men from Invermoriston wanted to go east to another kirkyard. A fight ensued in which several clansmen were killed and the survivors simply buried the body of the old dear where she lay. A small upright stone beside the road at Livisie is said to mark the location of her grave.

Such rammies were by no means confined to the Highlands. On 30 January 1699, the funeral took place of Lady Anne Hall, wife of

Sir James Hall of Dunglass in East Lothian, at the old church near her home. This was attended by crowds of the local nobility. A quarrel broke out between the coachmen of the Earls of Lothian and Roxburgh over precedence – which of their lordships' coaches should lead the way – and was 'very near engaging their masters'. It appears that the two nobs were hoping for promotion in the peerage, and were therefore 'rendered more irritable'. Whether anyone remembered Lady Anne in the midst of all this nonsense is not recorded.

FIBS

In the burgh records of the ancient royal burgh of Dumbarton is found the following terse note:

> On March 14, 1634 Margaret Hamilton was banist (banished) the toun for lying, in sa far as sche socht help to buy a mourning sheit for her deid bairne, when Sche had no bairne deid.

Praise the Lord and Pass the Speaking Trumpet - Faith isn't always the answer when eternity beckons. Confronted in 1831 by abundant death on his doorstep a Paisley minister wasn't taking any chances. In fear and trembling of a cholera outbreak he built a high paling around his home and communicated with the outside world using a bell and a speaking trumpet.

FIREWORKS

A man who is leading the way in providing fun departures for Scots is inventor and furniture maker Jon Nowell from Cockburnspath in

Berwickshire. He has already brought Scotland bookcases and wardrobes which can be converted with ease into coffins. He decided a few years ago that coffins should be as much for life as for death and his wardrobes only need the handles added, the lid put on and the lining placed inside – and you're ready to go. This year, in conjunction with a Sheffield fireworks manufacturer and Chinese consultants, he plans to offer the opportunity for Scots to be seen off in spectacular style, their ashes reverently placed inside fireworks and launched into the bright blue yonder.

The point of sale will be at crematoriums and the idea would be that only a token consignment of ashes would be sent up at a specially arranged family get-together – a post-cremation celebration, a classy wee send off, in fact. It is likely that the rockets will retail at £30 but it is most decidedly a one-off event and the rocket might be fired from any location, a cliff or mountain top, any spot to which the deceased was emotionally attached.

Jon does not see the idea spreading to other types of fireworks so we are unlikely to see adverts in the style of Spin Granny into Eternity with a Memorial Catherine Wheel! He is convinced the rocket idea will catch on: 'It will be a nice way for people to give their relatives a happy, colourful send-off. It will make funerals more like a celebration of the person's life rather than a drab sombre affair.' Jon also stresses the symbolic nature of the idea of folk being given a wee helping hand on the flight path to heaven.

FIRST OF SO MANY

The first soldier to be killed in the Great War – on 22 August 1914 – was Lieutenant George Thompson of the Royal Scots. He was fatally wounded in Africa while on attachment with the Gold Coast Regiment.

First Word

Superstition and the fear of damnation and death could make life gey complex in centuries past. The strange tradition of 'first word' provides an example. In Perthshire older folk would pass you by in silence and with a scowl if you had managed to get in the 'first word' with them. To pre-empt such an event they would often shout a greeting or a remark from a ridiculous distance.

Flags

If, like me, you are always baffled about the way flags on Scottish public buildings seem to shoot up and down from full mast to half-mast for no apparent reason, then here is the solution. The general rule is that flags should be flown at half-mast:

† from the announcement of the death of the British king or queen up to and including the day of their funeral
† on the funeral days of members of the Royal Family
† on the funeral days of foreign rulers, prime ministers and ex-prime ministers
† on special days as specifically directed by the monarch – e.g., on the loss of a great public figure or a national disaster

The bloke at the bottom of the guy rope has serious problems when a half-mast day coincides with a traditional flag-flying day such as a royal birthday. Generally, on such confusing, conflicting occasions, flags are flown in the normal manner.

FLATTERY

There Lies One who neither Feared nor Flattered Flesh
Words said to be spoken by Regent Morton
over the grave of John Knox

FLOWERS

Since antiquity flowers have been a staple in the rituals and superstitions surrounding the disposal of the dead. The life that the blossoms represent act as a vibrant counterpoint to the death that is being acknowledged. A prehistoric grave in Iraq was found to have contained pollen of eight different flowers.

After a fragrant survey of the flower shops of Scotland I can offer a few interesting insights into the current use of wreaths and flowers at Scottish funerals.

The most popular funeral flowers for wreaths and sprays have not changed much over the years but the big hit at the moment at least north of the Border, is the Victorian thistle which is usually backgrounded with white and draped with tartan. Most common basic blooms used in making up floral funeral tributes are chrysanthemums and gypsophila (known popularly as baby's breath). Apart from the thistles, white lilies, red roses and carnations remain favourites.

As far as the motifs which florists are asked to create for the dear departed, the most popular are names, 'Dad' and 'Mum', initials and occasionally nicknames. Cars and motor bikes, tractors and even quad bikes are regularly requested and for children creations include trains and teddy bears. One Borders florist was asked recently to produce a Pokémon character for a child's funeral.

Sometimes the requests are baffling. One northern florist recalled having been recently asked by a family for a sports car motif. The recipient was a young man who had killed himself by wrapping his machine round a telegraph pole. Strange. In Angus, I was told of the old farm servant who had always spoken of owning a limousine after he retired. He never did but his co-workers chipped in for a limousine-shaped spray that went with the old boy on the journey to his last resting place.

The corner-shop florists do look to have a future in the funeral business despite the advent of vast flower stalls in the local super-markets. One florist told me, 'We are interested in the people who have passed away. We want to help the family make a very personal tribute to the deceased. One-to-one service will hopefully always be more appealing than the ranks of anonymous bouquets in the superstores.'

FOREIGN FAREWELLS

Death, of course, is not unique to the Scots. To let you see that the oddest statistics and strangest events attach themselves to the most serious moment in life wherever you happen to live, I offer these snippets:

† Someone with more time on their hands than is healthy has calculated that you are more likely to be killed by a champagne cork than a poisonous spider.

† The public morgue in the Bronx district of New York is sometimes so busy that relatives are given numbered tickets and asked to queue prior to identifying their deceased family member.

† The first person to die of radiation poisoning was Marie Curie, discoverer of radium, who failed to take any precautions against radiation. Her notebooks are said to be still too hot to handle.

† Adrian IV, England's only Pope, choked to death on a fly while the Roman Emperor Claudius is said to have suffered a similar fate, choking on a feather being used by a physician to promote vomiting.

† After the Battle of Trafalgar, Nelson's body was brought back to England in a barrel of rum to slow decomposition.

FORENSIC MASTERWORK

The identification of all but six of the 259 passengers on Pan-Am 301, which was blown up over Lockerbie in Dumfriess-shire in 1988, is still regarded as a miracle of forensic investigation. Body parts were scattered over an 845 square mile area.

FORESIGHT

One of the first tasks for a new Scottish bride in centuries past was to prepare her own shroud and that of her husband. You'll hear it said that this was to remind her of her mortality but you can't help thinking that it is more likely to have been the canny far-seeing Scot simply being provident.

FORGERS

New Year's Eve, 1567 witnessed the execution of a burgess of Dundee called Robert Jack for the crime of counterfeiting coins. There is a widely-held perception, which has lasted through to the present day, that judges believe that crimes against establishment are more deserving of the death sentence than those against the person. And it seems to have been borne out by Jack's demise – this pillar of the local community was hanged and his body was quartered thereafter.

FORGETFULNESS

With tremendous quantities of drink being consumed at funerals of the gentry in seventeenth- and eighteenth-century Scotland, it is perhaps no surprise to learn that there are a number of recorded instances of half-cut mourners forgetting to take along the corpse when the time came for the burial. In the early 1700s, at the funeral of Mrs Forbes of Culloden, her son Duncan, later to become the Lord President of the Court of Session, 'conducted the festivities'. Copious quantities of drink were taken but finally the word was given for the 'lifting' of the coffin and everyone rose to head for the burial ground.

The gentlemen unsteadily clambered aboard their cuddies and the common rabble staggered in the general direction of the kirkyard. Arriving at the graveside, there was general bewilderment on the discovery that Mrs Forbes had been left behind. A small party was sent back to 'bring on' the corpse and there were a few red faces, not only from the drink, when the deceased was belatedly lowered into her grave.

This forgetfulness was by no means unique. In Berwickshire in the mid eighteenth century, Mrs Home of Billie had to be 'retrieved' after the company took too much refreshment. And, in Orkney, in the mid nineteenth century, a tipsy funeral party allowed a coffin to topple into a burn in spate and it was carried downstream before it could be retrieved from the middle of a loch.

FORTITUDE

John Graham of Claverhouse, Viscount Dundee, is seen by some to be a dashing chevalier – a royalist in the mode of The Marquis of Montrose. Truth to tell the Covenanting times were a desperately bloody business which left little room for gallantry and 'Bluidy Clavers', as he was dubbed, was a tough cookie. Having murdered a fugitive in front of his family, Claverhouse is said to have asked the woman, pointing to the corpse, 'And what think ye of your husband now?'

The brave answer came, 'I aye thought much o' him and now mair than ever.'

FUN

By the eighteenth century, funerals were reckoned to be Dunfermline's favourite pastime – closely followed by weddings . . . and cockfighting.

David Hatton of Dysart in Fife is probably best remembered as the nineteenth-century eccentric who tried to open a thread mill using 10,000 'little pedestrians' – house mice which would turn the mill's treadmill wheels. This project, surprise, surprise, never got off the ground but he had more success with a much simpler, if macabre, endeavour. He exhibited a coffin, a penny being charged for a look at the accommodation which the vast majority of people would only have contact with under the most trying of circumstances – a death in the family. But, wait for it. For an extra penny the visitor was allowed to clamber into the casket and get a flavour of eternity in their 'long, last home'. After Hatton moved from Dunfermline to Thornton in mid Fife, his coffin display became more popular than ever although, when showing his patrons 'how the coffin fitted', he always rejected pleas from the enthusiasts to have the lid screwed down on them. Bizarre folk those Fifers, eh? On the evening of 12 March 1851, the screws were, however, finally brought into use as Davie was cairted off for burial in his own, beloved black box.

This is not a uniquely Scottish experience. In the same period in the United States a woman had a casket specially designed and built and set up in her front room. When friends called round she would climb in so they could see how splendid she would look when laid out. How's that for a fun afternoon out?

FUNERAL ANTHEMS (CONTEMPORARY)

According to a survey conducted by the Co-operative Funeral Service a year or two back, the top ten favourite funeral anthems are:

1. 'Wind Beneath my Wings' – Bette Midler
2. 'My Heart Will Go On' – Celine Dion
3. 'I Will Always Love You' – Whitney Houston
4. 'The Best' – Tina Turner
5. 'Angels' – Robbie Williams

6. 'You'll Never Walk Alone' – Gerry and the Pacemakers
7. 'Candle in the Wind' – Elton John
8. 'Unchained Melody' – The Righteous Brothers
9. 'Bridge over Troubled Waters' – Simon and Garfunkel
10. 'Time to Say Goodbye' – Sarah Brightman

This is just a sample of a whole new genre of funeral melodies which also include John Lennon's 'Imagine' and 'Let It Be' and George Harrison's 'My Sweet Lord'. But probably the most bizarre is the Village People classic, 'YMCA'. A spokeswoman for the Co-op explained this growing phenomenon thus: 'Perhaps mourners want to recreate the emotion of their favourite films and ensure their loved ones receive a funeral worthy of a star.'

This fusion of funerals with pop culture is part of the wider trend examined elsewhere in the book as reflecting the desire to broaden the personal aspects of funerals where religion no longer plays such a significant part. In truth, fifty years ago funerals were a doddle for the undertaker but things are changing. With tens of thousands of specially-requested melodies played at funerals nationally, it is now clear that songs which seem to others to be simply bizarre can have a very special, highly personal significance for the bereaved.

Twentieth-century Scots poet Norman MacCaig caught the flavour and mystery of the Highland funeral hauntingly from the point of the deceased in his work 'Every Day':

What's that cart that nobody sees
Grinding along the shore road?

Whose is the horse that pulls it, the white horse
That bares its yellow teeth to the wind?

They turn, unnoticed by anyone,
Into the field of slanted stones.

My friends meet me. They lift me from the cart and,
The greetings over, we go smiling underground.

FUNERAL ANTHEMS (QUIRKY)

† 'Stairway to Heaven'
† 'Give Me Oil in my Lamp, Keep me Burning'
† 'Living in a Box'
† 'Going Underground'
† 'Burn, Baby Burn (Disco Inferno)'
† 'Wake Me Up Before You Go-Go'
† 'Another One Bites the Dust'
† 'Crawl Back Under Your Stone'
† 'Smoke Gets in Your Eyes'
† 'Firestarter'

And many a recent Scottish funeral has been enlivened, the tension
and stress thrown to the wind, with a last request from the deceased
for a couple of verses of that Ginger Rogers and Fred Astaire
Hollywood favourite, 'Dancing Cheek to Cheek'. It opens with the
appropriate, if perhaps over-optimistic, line, 'Heaven, I'm in Heaven.'

FUNERAL ANTHEMS (TRADITIONAL)

† 'Abide with Me'
† 'Amazing Grace'

† 'The Twenty-Third Psalm'
† 'Flower of Scotland'
† Pachelbel's 'Canon'
† 'Highland Cathedral'
† 'Ae Fond Kiss'

FUNERAL FROLICS

In February 1576, Madge Morison was fined for dressing up in men's clothing at a funeral. It seems that cross-dressing at funerals was a popular pastime among younger folk in the Granite City. As Gwyn Thomas suggested in the 1970s, a 'damn good funeral is still one of our best and cheapest acts of theatre'. There is also a lot of truth in the observation from George Ade that funerals in the city are simply an interruption to traffic while in the country they are a form of popular entertainment.

FUNERALS

On the day of the burial people arrived long before the hour of the 'lifting' and, in rural areas, out in the barn, tables would be spread with meat, bread, cheese and whisky aplenty. Once under way, the coffin was carried in relays and, if an inn was to be passed, a halt was called. (*See* **Cairns**) Free-for-all fights were common, pallbearers were regularly unable to keep their feet and often the coffin suffered serious damage by being dropped. Passing into another parish, men from the other side would be waiting to claim the coffin 'with something akin to the avidity of beasts of prey'. Inter-parish scraps,

A Highland Funeral – artist Sir James Guthrie (1882) (courtesy of Glasgow Museums and Libraries)

as we've seen already, were frequent, particularly at these handovers.

Funeral parties even walked from Glenshee over to Braemar and, one occasion, in the 1700s, is recalled when the Glenshee group were met at the top of the Cairnwell by a party from Braemar. The Glenshee men became aggressive, clearly intending to start a rammy. They were brought to their senses by one of their number, Farquharson of Auchendryne, who warned them that 'if they did not desist the result would be that wheras they had brought one corpse, they would be taking back three'.

Many villains and much-hated individuals populate the annals of Scotland. However, few were so detested that dead dogs were flung into their graves. Colonel Francis Charteris was born around the year 1699. He so outraged the sensibilities of decent folk with his depraved and self-indulgent behaviour that he was attacked in writings by both John Arbuthnot and Alexander Pope.

According to the latter this 'paragon of wickedness' was infamous for all the vices. His army career ended abruptly when he was drummed out of his regiment for being a cheat. He was banned from the towns of Brussels and Ghent for similar dishonesty. After 'a hundred tricks' at the gaming table he took to moneylending and quickly amassed a fortune. He was twice convicted of rape and, in the eyes of many, was a veritable son of Satan. Arbuthnot wrote a classic epitaph in which he spoke of the insatiable avarice and the undeviating depravity of the man.

A few 'friends' did attend his funeral but they had to defend themselves with swords from the furious mob who, as well as throwing dead dogs, tried to tear the body from the coffin.

GATEWATCHERS

One curious superstition related to death, which is found from Mull to Aberdeenshire, is a belief that the spirit of the last person buried keeps watch over the churchyard until the next burial. The job is looked upon, unsurprisingly, as a being very undesirable and this sometimes led to unpleasant scenes. When two deaths occurred on the same day in the same neighbourhood, there was often great rivalry to see which body could be interred first. On one occasion, two processions were closing on the kirkyard from different directions and, seeing each other in the distance, the two parties stepped up their pace. The funeral group who were closer broke into a gallop and, to consolidate their lead as they reached the kirkyard dyke, they threw the coffin containing the body of an old woman o'er the dyke and reached the grave first. At this point, a wee boy belonging to the successful party is said to have clapped his hands and shouted, 'Chosuinn m shean-mhathair an reise!' – 'Granny's won the race!' I feel sure the old dear must have been delighted to be hustled into eternity.

GHOST

This is a restless, disembodied spirit – a bit like our sense of Scottishness which wanders the globe looking for the new Caledonia. Like the wraith, Scots may find that contentment lies far closer to home than they ever imagined.

GLUTTONS

Overeating was a rare vice in medieval Scotland where starvation was a much more common experience. However, one exception who very much proved the rule was the obese Douglas Earl James, who, on his death in 1443, was found to have four stones of tallow in his stomach. Maybe he was just big-boned.

GNASHERS

Black Ewen of Lochiel was a larger than life Hielandman. It's said that, in 1654, on his discovering government soldiers cutting down trees on his land for the construction of Fort William, a major set-to ensued. Clansmen and government troops locked together in a fight to the death and, during the clash, he sank his teeth into the throat of an English trooper – quickly ending the scrap. Later, Black Ewen was to describe it as 'the sweetest bite I ever tasted'.

GOOD GUYS

Wandering through Scotland's graveyards and glancing at the tombstones, it does seem that in death everyone is a hero or heroine, a fine parent, servant to the community, master craftsman, regular churchgoer, etc., etc. It is reasonable to ask, 'Where are all the bad guys?' or, as the writer Charles Lamb once remarked to his sister on walking away from a graveyard as a child, 'Mary, where are all the naughty people buried?'

GRAMMAR

You will find crematoria, crematoriums and crematories as plurals used to describe the building in which cremation takes place. Never, ever make the mistake of describing this location as the creamery.

GRANNY SAID IT

There is no need to be afraid of ghosts. If the living did as little harm as the dead, the world would be a better place.

GRAVE ROBBERS

See **Bodysnatchers**

GRAVESTONES

See **Tombstones**

GRAVEYARDS

It has proved impossible to get an accurate figure for the number of graveyards in Scotland. Best estimates seem to point to the remarkable total of at least 5,000 either still in use or closed for business. These include our vast urban graveyards down to small enclosures on remote islands. The density of graveyards also varies from region to region. While some smaller local authorities geographically have responsibility for a handful of cemeteries, Aberdeenshire has over 800 burial grounds in its care.

GREEN BURIALS

The numbers remain small but increasingly green, or woodland, burials are finding favour with Scots who seek an environmentally gentle conclusion to their existence.

Worries over cremation gases and overcrowding in cemeteries has led most of Scotland's local authorities to open or seriously consider green burial sites. And private green burial grounds are also springing up across the country. In them, people can be laid to rest in cardboard coffins, their graves marked only by a tree or clumps of flowers. Edinburgh, Dundee, East Dunbartonshire, Midlothian, Dumfries and Galloway, South Ayrshire and Renfrewshire are among the authorities offering this facility. These woodland sites, bright with wild flowers and populated by songbirds, are in sharp contrast with the cramped conditions of most Victorian yards. One of the reasons the idea has not caught hold more forcibly seems to be that only one person can be buried in each grave. And partners often wish to be buried with each other. As ways of dealing with death slowly change, the cheaper option of a woodland burial seems likely to have more appeal. But even this seemingly sound environmental technique of despatching the dead can bring its problems. The Natural Death Centre in London discovered that symbolic clouds of balloons released at green funerals may be a potential threat to marine carnivores who mistake the floating rubber for jellyfish.

GRIEVANCES

Drowning was a common enough cause of death around the rugged West Coast of Scotland but the deceased hanging around to annoy the local populace post-mortem was a less frequent happening. The body of an English sailor was once washed ashore at Kiloran Bay on Colonsay and buried by local folk beside a stream near the shore. His ghost then unnervingly started to waylay people as they passed back and forwards to Balnahard at the northern tip of the island. The ghost was of a mean disposition, it seems – one man with whom it shook hands lost the use of his arm. Another man who was carrying a gun was asked by the wraith to hand over the weapon. However, warned by the first man's experience, he refused and threatened to blow the ghost's spectral brains oot. The ghost suddenly became the essence of reasonableness and explained that the waters of the stream had undermined the bank and exposed his bones to the elements, hence his restlessness. The ex-sailor undertook not to trouble the locals again if the bones were transferred to a dry grave. This was done and the spot is still marked by a loose cairn at the foot of Cnoc Ingibrig, Balavetchy.

ONE MAN'S VISION

Psychologists generally agree that there is a crucial need to find an outlet for grief. In the Victorian era, sex was the great taboo but, in twentieth-century Scotland, this was replaced by the distancing of people from death. (*See* **Introduction**) In an increasingly secular world, a new approach is taking shape. David MacColl is Cemeteries Services Manager for North Ayrshire Council and President of the Institute of Cemetery and Crematorium Management, a national organisation of some 700 members, mostly local authorities, from across the country. A son of the manse, he believes that the cemeteries must become accessible community assets and, looking ahead over the next half century, sees no reason why recreational facilities should not sit side by side with last resting places.

Alexander Solzhenitsyn, the great Russian novelist, wrote that the presence of the dead among the living will be a daily fact in any society which encourages its people to live. D J Enright also sees cemeteries as places of common and relaxed resort. And David MacColl believes that the more insightful of death carers are now convinced that if, as a nation, we are to rediscover a more comfortable and compassionate approach to death, then choice must be put back into the manner of dying. If people want to die at home, they should be allowed to do so despite the complications that this might involve. Where is the dignity in death, he asks, when your final certificate does not carry the address where you might have lived for sixty years but, instead, that of a care home, hospital or hospice where you spent the final months or merely weeks of your life?

It is also important, says David, that people must have the opportunity to deal with the death of a loved one if so desired. If you would rather leave it to the professionals, then that, of course, is another option. He also points out that some towns and villages might not have major parks or communal sites where people can walk around but they will almost certainly have a cemetery. 'I would encourage people to try to use the cemetery to re-establish a sense of community and enjoy the aesthetic and historical appeal of these sites. After all a cemetery is an open book on the history of the community.'

It's a long road and some would say that burial grounds can never again form the kind of vibrant part of the community as they did in yesteryear with fairs among the lairs. However, there are combined historical and nature walks already taking place through our Scottish cemeteries. Realistically, boneyards and recreational facilities still seem worlds apart in the modern perception but who knows? Attitudes can change rapidly these days.

GUILT

Throughout his adult life James IV wore an iron chain round his waist as a penance for his part in his father's murder at Sauchieburn in 1488. Each year, he added extra links to keep the memory of his crime fresh.

HALLOWE'EN

Based on a Celtic Festival marking the start of winter, Hallowe'en was designed, quite literally, to raise the spirits of the tribe at a time when the leaves withered and died, forest creatures went into hiding and, worst of all, the sun was disappearing for longer periods into the strange world below the horizon. It was seen historically as a time when the barriers with the other world were lowered. *Samhain* was the name adopted by the Celtic peoples for this party.

Why did people dress up? One theory suggests that people disguised themselves as spirits of the dead. The reason for this, according to Greg Palmer, was that real spirits passing by would believe they were seeing their colleagues working a particular neighbourhood and move on to more productive territory. In his studies of Orkney folklore, Ernest Marwick came across the following unflattering description of a group of Northern Isles guizers in the 1880s:

> . . . they stood like so many statues . . . they kept up an incessant
> grunt, grunt, grunt, or a noise partly resembling swine and turkey

cock . . . they were veiled and their head dresses or caps were about eighteen inches in height made of straw twisted and plaited. The spirits, for such they appeared to be, had long staves with which they kept rapping on the floor. Between them and the door stood one as black as Horni [the Devil] but more resembling a human being than any of the others. His head dress was a Souwester and he carried a creel on his back.

Hallowe'en was also a time for peering into the future and various techniques were used. My own favourite by a long mile was for a young man to remove his clothing, name the last person to be buried in the kirkyard and declare, 'Keep doo dis till I come back.' He then pushed his head into the nearest midden where he confidently expected to see a vision of the future. Strong stuff, that home brew!

HARD FACTS

Most people in Scotland now die without a family member being present. In the upper, middle and professional classes it is said to be rare for the nearest and dearest to be present at these last moments. However, the lower the social class, the more likely it is for the bereaved to be there at the end. It is also the upper, middle and professional who have most speedily abandoned the clothes of mourning.

Haste

In some cultures the procession to the grave is carried out without stopping in case a dissatisfied spirit escapes from the body and haunts survivors.

Headstones

See **Tombstones**

Hearses and Horses

By the 1860s, the hearse had made its appearance even in the rural areas, as a description from Knapdale indicates. Two black horses normally drew the hearse. On the roof, a number of black plumes waved in the wind. The driver of the hearse had attached to his hat a long tail of black crêpe, reaching halfway down his back. All the male relatives of the deceased, even young boys, wore a band of white linen round the cuffs of their coats or jackets. They also wore a white tie and had a band of crêpe round their caps. For at least a month or six weeks after the funeral, these emblems of mourning continued to be worn when attending church on Sundays.

The most famous surviving horse-drawn hearse is to be found in the Royal Scottish Museum in Edinburgh and dates from 1785. It was used in the East Lothian village of Bolton and its most famous occupants were members of the family of Robert Burns.

The Funeral of Thomas Carlyle – artist Robert Weir Allan (courtesy of Glasgow Museums and Libraries)

HEART-RENDING

Robert Bruce, patriot king of Scotland, always wanted to go on the Crusades. But the struggles to make Scotland free took a lot of his spare time and he died with his wish unfulfilled. Step up his old pal Jimmy Douglas who took the king's heart into battle against the Moors in Spain. He is even said to have lobbed the monarch's heart at the enemy. The relic of Bruce eventually found its way back to Scotland and was placed in Melrose Abbey. This story remained very much in the 'Aye, right' category until the body of the king was exhumed in 1818 and his rib cage was found to have been sawn through, suggesting that, right enough, his heart had been removed.

HEATING

The crematorium at Leamington Spa in Warwickshire was the first to be fitted with a heat exchange unit. This uses the reheating of gases created by cremation to heat a water tank which, in turn, heats the crematorium.

HELL

For most Scots, there are only vague notions about who is likely to end up in the fiery pit as a guest of Auld Nick. Basically, we believe it to be the destination for everybody who annoys, intimidates, betrays or badmouths us. However, Buddhist philosophy gives a much more precise idea of what to expect. Awaiting serious sinners is a whole range of punishments but, interestingly, this is not a forever-and-a-day situation which seems to be the suggestion in the

Christian way o' things.

Of particular interest to the Scots might be the following:

Name	Crime	Duration
Black Rope Hell		
(*Kala-Sutra*)	stealing	1,000 years
Crowded Hell		
(*Samghata*)	abusing sex	2,000 years
Screaming Hell		
(*Raurava*)	drunkenness	4,000 years
Burning Heat Hell		
(*Avici*)	not believing in Hell	16,000 years

Oddly, killers need only expect 500 years in the Hell of Repetition (*Samjiva*). A different set of values operating there, I would suggest.

HEROES AND HEROINES

Every kirkyard has its own remarkable stories to tell. It is the history of ordinary people who generally lived their lives within sight of the church – ordinary, unremarkable lives, filled with love and trouble, a simple and straightforward existence. In many ways these lives are very different from the ones we lead today – and, yet, in many ways, they are quite similar. These people, however, were reconciled to spending eternity in their home turf. It was the fulfilment of life.

Gravestones can tell you some of the story. Take John Christie, a seventy-year-old man who, according to his headstone in Arbroath Abbey churchyard, lost his life on 24 September 1785 while acting as a post-rider between Dundee and Arbroath.

A bit of research unveils the full, moving story. The night in question was wild, wet and windy when John, a post-rider for decades, arrived with the mailbags at the Ford of Elliot. In the downpour, the normally placid stream had become a torrent. The folk at the ford cottages advised him to take the long way round which would have added two miles to the journey. But old John was having none of it. The mail had to go through. He headed his trusty old horse into the flow and the hardy animal made it with a struggle to the other bank. But sadly John was swept away, his body being discovered next morning at the mouth of the river. His death led, within a year, to the construction of a bridge at Elliot.

In Broughty Ferry, in 1867, the council decided to order the closure of the overcrowded and insanitary old burying ground after an outbreak of cholera had killed twelve people. Great opposition was expressed, however, by the fisherfolk who held the graveyard in great reverence, regarding it as their sacred ground. They defied the council orders and found a champion in seventy-year-old bellman and gravedigger William Skirving, who was excessively proud of his position as gravedigger and felt that he personally should have been served with the closure order, in order that he could contest it in his own name. So Willie continued to open graves for the fisherfolk to bury their dead in the family lair.

As the defiance continued, the magistrates decided to act and, after another illegal burial was reported, Willie was summoned before the Sheriff in Dundee and fined £5 with the alternative of two months in prison. A subscription was immediately taken up and, in the space of an hour, the fiver was collected. The money came principally from amongst the fishers who organised a procession, met their hero at the railway station, carried him shoulder high in triumph to a tavern at the beach, where he was liberally regaled, and finally escorted him home.

126

Elsewhere the closure of old burial grounds in the Victorian era caused problems. At Kirriemuir in 1858, the old burial ground was found to be in an 'unwholesome condition' and again the council ordered the burials should be discontinued forthwith. The first tombstone in the new ground, an old quarry hole, did not halt the murmurings of discontent amongst the townsfolk. One 'old malcontent' declared, as she drew her dying breath, that she would 'never gang tae lie there'. Her son was no great comfort in this situation declaring, 'Dinna fash yerself, mither, you'll no' have to gang there, we'll just drive ye there!'

HOORAY HENRY

The death of Henry Lord Darnley, husband of Mary, Queen of Scots and king by marriage, has intrigued historians and historical novelists alike for centuries. The tale of his slaying at Kirk o' Field in Edinburgh has been retold a hundred times. No version, to my mind at least, recaptures the stark, matter-of-fact contemporary report that appears in the *Diurnal of Occurents* which was republished by the Bannatyne Club in 1833.

> . . . at two in the morning, there came certain traitors to the provost's house, wherein was our sovereign's husband Henry, and ane servant of his, callit William Taylor, lying in their naked beds; and there privily with wrong keys openit the doors, and come in upon the said prince, and there without mercy worried him and his said servant in their beds; and thereafter took him and his servant furth of that house and cuist him naked in ane yard beside The Thief Raw, and syne come to the house again, and blew the

house in the air, sae that there remainit not ane stane upon the other, undestroyit . . . at five hours, the said Prince and his servant was found lying dead in said yard, and was ta'en into ane house in the Kirk of Field and laid there while they were buriet.

Knifed, strangled, blown up. Somebody was intent on ensuring that Henry Lord Darnley was not going to walk away from Kirk o' Field.

HOPE

Perhaps my favourite quip on the theme of death features three friends killed together in a car crash. While waiting at the pearly gates for St Peter to get out of his kip, they get round to discussing what they would like to hear as their friends gather around the coffins for the funeral. The first casualty, in no doubt, says he would like to hear them declare that he was one of the most talented musicians of his generation and a great family man. The second of the trio is equally confident, hoping to hear his ability as a teacher praised and the view expressed that he had helped shape a better future for the children he came into contact with. The third man, looking nervously around, replies, 'I'd just like to hear them say . . . Look! He's Moving!!'

HORSEMAN (HEADLESS)

The headless horseman is a bit of a supernatural cliché but Scotland has several splendid examples of this spooky phenomenon, the most spectacular perhaps being on Mull, where his appearance is said to signal the death of a member of the local McLean family. This noted harbinger of doom is the cranially challenged Hugh of Little Head – so little, in fact, that he's missing it altogether. This napperless horseman is said to make his appearance whenever any of the MacLeans of Loch Buie on Mull are nearing the end of the road. On the eve of a battle, Hugh met the spirit most often seen before death. This was the washerwoman and she would be found beside a stream washing the shrouds of those about to die. He asked his fate and was told he would die unless his wife gave him butter without being asked for it. She did not and, at the end of a clan battle, Hugh of the Little Head was decapitated and his black horse galloped away with the corpse still in the saddle. Since then he has appeared on the road beside Loch Scridain, as a herald of imminent death.

That most haunted of cities, Edinburgh, has an unusual spin on this form of haunting. The Death Coach is said to rattle up the Royal Mile hauled by a team of headless cuddies.

HOSPITALITY

Kenneth MacAlpin, the man who gets the credit for forcing the warring Scots and Picts together in the 800s into the first version of the multifaceted place we call Scotland, is also the man who brought a whole new meaning to the phrase 'dropping in for dinner'. Legend has it that Ken decided it was necessary to dispose of a particularly awkward bunch of Pictish noblemen in his quest to unite Scotland. He invited them to a feast at Scone and, at the end of the beano, bolts beneath the tables were released, tipping the half-cut diners into a pit where they were put to the sword.

How Some Foreign Magnates Snuffed It

George II – reported to have fallen off the toilet pan and banged his napper

Charles VIII of France – bashed his head on an overhead beam

Alexandros I of Greece – received a fatal bite from his pet monkey

Claudius, Emperor of Rome – choked on a feather (don't ask!)

Henry I – his passion for lampreys, small eels, was his downfall

Alexander the Great – dropped dead during a drinking contest

Haakon VII of Norway– slipped in the bath and struck his head on the taps

Attila the Hun – burst a blood vessel cavorting with one of his twelve wives

King John of England – overdid the peaches in cider at a Norfolk beano

Pope Alexander VI – died having swallowed poison intended for his cardinals

How Some Scottish Monarchs Died

Duncan I (1034–1040) – slain by his rival Macbeth

Macbeth (1040–1057) – slain by his rival Malcolm Canmore, etc., etc., etc.

Alexander II (1214–1249) – died near Oban while trying to bring the Highlands to heel

Alexander III (1249–1286) – his cuddy failed to take a cliff-top corner at Kinghorn

Margaret of Norway (1286–1290) – died of seasickness in Orkney

Robert I (1306–1329) – the wasting disease of leprosy finally did for the patriot king

Robert III (1390–1406) – collapsed and died on hearing his son James was an English prisoner

James I (1406–1437) – ventilated by his dagger-wielding nobility after a tennis match

James II (1437–1460) – blown up by his own cannon at Roxburgh Castle

James V (1513–1542) – took a fatal huff after his defeat at Solway Moss

HOW TO SHRINK A HUMAN HEAD IN TEN EASY STEPS

1. Remove head from the body – carefully allowing for a good length of neck.
2. Slit skin from the nape of the neck to the forehead.
3. Push skin carefully from back of the head towards the centre of the face.
4. Remove the skull and jaw.
5. Sew the eyes and mouth closed.
6. Boil for two hours in a saucepan until the flesh falls away from the skin.
7. Dry the skin and allow it to cool slowly.
8. Sew the skin up from nape of neck to forehead.

9. Heat river pebbles, fill the head with pebbles and sand and shape as required.
10. Smoke overnight above the campfire.

HUBBLE BUBBLE

There's a line from that splendiferous Gilbert and Sullivan opera, *The Mikado*, which has remained with me even forty years after my stumbling role as a Gentleman of Japan in Clydebank High School's end-of-term extravaganza. In the midst of all the hanky-panky with Nanky-Poo and the Three Little Maids, a discussion takes place on the merits of various forms of execution – something lingering, with boiling oil in it, is suggested. Now G&S were simply exploiting the Japanese reputation in such sinister matters. But Scots should not be too critical – north of the Border we were no slouches in the dirty-tricks department and were not averse to boiling up our fellow countrymen as a means of administering 'justice'.

Scottish criminal records do show instances – probably fairly rare cases, it has to be admitted – of individuals being boiled alive. In one notable episode, a medieval counterfeiter in Edinburgh met this horrendous fate. On reflection, it's really no surprise to discover that the Scots, who perfected the art of tearing a body limb from limb using carthorses and who became skilled tormentors during the witch frenzies, were also adept in cooking up mischief in the cauldron.

Surely the most remarkable instance is reported in the fifteenth-century affair of the 'Boiled Sheriff of the Mearns'. The incident led to the lawman, quite literally, becoming Kincardineshire's most famous soup du jour. In the early 1400s, Melville of Glenbervie was recognised throughout the north-east as one of the harshest law officers ever to sit in judgement over his fellow Scots. Many complaints about him found their way to James I who, in one moment of uncharacteristic impatience during an audience, declared, 'Sorrow gin the Sheriff were soddin' and supped in broo.' According to the records of the encounter, the complainers were not at all fazed by the king's exasperation – indeed, they left wearing wry smiles and probably the dastardly plot was already hatching.

Shortly afterwards, the lairds of Arbuthnott, Mather, Laurieston and Pittaraw decoyed Melville to the top of the Hill of Garvock above Laurencekirk on the pretext that he was to join a hunting expedition. On this spot, so we're told, which still carries the name of Sheriff's Pot, the lairds prepared a fire and cauldron into which Melville was plunged. After he was well and truly soddin', as per the king's recipe, the lairds actually partook of this 'hell's broth' just to ensure the royal mandate was carried out to the letter. Naturally the lairds were outlawed for this terrible act but the fact that they do not seem to have been pursued with utmost vigour might suggest embarrassment at court over the king's fatal remark which opened the door for one of the oddest slayings in the annals of Scotland.

Just one final point to ponder. Would you rather be boiled to death by being plunged directly into the boiling water or sat in the cauldron as the water temperature slowly rose round about you? Not something, thankfully, that many of us have consider these days.

Human Slipway

Norsemen, who were known to be tough customers at the best of times, are also thought to have indulged in a ceremony of ritual purification for new warships. The wild practice of dedicating new longships involved rolling them down to the sea over the bodies of sacrificial victims to redden the keels.

Human Weakness

They are lifeless who are faultless.

Hypothermia

Alcohol, as is well known, thins the blood. Hypothermia is that sinister, beguiling companion who stalks the chill places of this earth whispering seductively, 'You'll be fine – just close your eyes and have forty winks.' Together they make a deadly duo. We have tragic evidence of this effect during the bitterly cold winter of 1601/1602 when the deep freeze is reported to have lasted fully six months.

In the early part of the New Year there was a ten-day snowfall. The Earl of Sutherland was travelling with his party from Golspie through the Glen of Loth, ploughing through deep snow, when a fresh storm burst upon them, driving thick snow full in their faces. Reports of the incident say:

134

Some of the company drank aquavitae which by chance happened
to be there. This made them afterwards so feeble that they were
not able to endure against the storm.

The Earl and the bulk of his party stuck together and made it to
safety but some of the drinkers, including the Earl's harper, were
dispersed by the storm and were found frozen to death in the
morning. Several of the whisky drinkers were thought to have been
saved by being carried home on the shoulders of their comrades.

ILLNESS

If someone was regularly complaining about feeling unwell, they might be encouraged by the saying 'Ye're nae fae yet!' – which simply means they still had plenty of time before their encounter with the Grim Reaper.

IMBOWELLING

This is the quaint old Scottish word for embalming.

IMMORTALITY

Robert Blair was an Edinburgh-born preacher who studied in his native city and in Holland before taking up parish ministry in the 1730s at Athelstaneford in East Lothian. His claim to fame is as the author of a blank verse poem called 'The Grave', which introduced the so-called 'churchyard' school of poetry. He was a big fan of the natural world and, in particular, the science of botany. His poem was considered too heavyweight by several publishers but achieved fame when it was illustrated by William Blake. Part of the poem runs thus:

'Tis but a night, a long and moonless night,
We make the Grave our bed, and then are gone.
Thus, at the shut of ev'n, the weary bird
Leaves the wide air, and in some lonely brake
Cow'rs down, and dozes till the dawn of day,
Then claps his well-fledg'd wings, and bears away.

INDIVIDUALITY

One of the scariest aspects of death is surely the fact that, in dying, we relinquish everything that makes us individuals. It has been said that all the corpses in the world are chemically identical, but living individuals are most definitely not.

INSECTS

Kill a midge and a thousand relatives will turn up at the funeral!

INSTEAD OF DYING, GRANDAD HAS . . .

† Gone away on a long holiday, a very long holiday
† Gone to visit God

† Gone to a happy land, far, far away
† Gone to sleep
† Gone to heaven to see your granny
† Gone to the corner shop for cigarettes

INSURANCE

'Well, she didn't waste any time,' mused Mungo Barr, one half of the Duddingston and Nor' Loch Insurance Company of Edinburgh, as he contemplated the insurance claim on the life of James II, King of Scots. Mary of Gueldres, his queen, had dropped off the document while doing her Saturday morning shopping in the High Street.

The facts were straightforward enough – killed on 3 August 1460 by a bursting cannon; location, Roxburgh Castle; a timber wedge, used to tighten iron barrel hooks, struck him down; the cannon had probably been overfilled with gunpowder; death would have been instantaneous due to insured's proximity to the cannon. His love of artillery seemed to have killed the king – yet Mungo had a few nagging doubts.

'Aye, we better cough up the coin or she'll have the heavies round here before you can say Mons Meg.' His junior partner Tam Sheriff, scratched the back of his ear with his goose quill pen and watched the log crackle and spurt in the grate. For the pioneering insurance men it had been the ultimate coup – a royal insurance policy. It wasn't big money but it was a breakthrough. Naturally they had set high premiums, bearing in mind the violent pastimes of the Scots nobility, but the royal family had been anxious to be seen in the vanguard of this unusual form of investment.

Mungo pulled a dusty file marked 'Artillerie' in big bold script from under his desk. 'Look, Tam, I'd settle this in a minute but there are loose ends. I knew these damned cannons would be nothing but trouble.' He began to leaf through the sheets of parchment, reading aloud all the time and hinting at some dark conspiracy. Sheriff had the odd sensation of cold steel on the nape of his neck. He'd given up a well-paid job as the hangman's assistant for a career in insurance. Maybe it hadn't been such a good idea.

As early as 1384, according to Mungo's notes, Robert II had ordered up a gun. Only £4 had been paid for this piece of equipment, according to the Exchequer Rolls, but it had been the start of a whole new war game. In the last year of his reign, James I had spent nearly £600 on artillery – nobility's latest deadly toy.

The contemporary material was intriguing. Strange coincidences linked James to the instrument of his death. The bombard that killed the monarch was called The Lion, the symbol of the Scottish throne, and it arrived in Scotland from the Low Countries in 1430, the year of the king's birth, possibly as a christening present. In a tragic irony, a verse had been engraved on The Lion outlining the marvellous deeds it would perform for the young prince. And it was true – apart from Mons Megs, it had no equal at dingin' doon castles.

Yet, even before its arrival, there was an ominous omen. Crossing the North Sea, it broke loose in the hold and smashed a cask of best wine. Then there was Mary of Gueldres who actively encouraged James's interest in guns, even bringing some weapons to Scotland as part of her dowry – odd connections aplenty but all circumstantial, nothing concrete.

Slamming the folder shut in a cloud of stour, Mungo declared, 'We'll have to pay up. But we're getting rid of that soothsayer and we're hiking up the premiums. What wi' his faither getting himself knifed at Perth and now this, thae Stewarts are beginning to look like a bad risk.'

Around 1700 in England it was possible to buy an insurance policy which protected you from going straight to Hell.

Interesting Thoughts on Death

The human race is the only one that knows it must die, and it knows this only through experience. A child brought up alone and transported to a desert island would have no more idea of death than a cat or a plant.

Voltaire, Frenchman and philosopher

If we were to live here always, with no other care than how to feed, clothe and house ourselves, life would be a very sorry business. It is immeasurably heightened by the solemnity of death.

Alexander Smith, Scotsman and writer

Death and the sun are not to be looked at steadily.

La Rochefoucauld, Frenchman and writer

Intoxication

Drink, or more accurately the abuse of drink, remains one of Scotland's greatest killers. That this has been the way o' things for at the very least two centuries is evidenced by a report from *The Glasgow Herald* of 7 January 1820. The newspaper reported some painful occurrences in the previous week 'in consequence of intemperate use of spirituous liquors'. One woman with a drink in her in the city fell into a fire and was burned 'in a manner too shocking for description'. In a kindly footnote, the paper notes, 'Another was found dead. A well-known semi-idiot, Dog Kate, was found in a state of insensibility . . . and was carried to the police office where she died in a few hours. Her death is attributed to the bad quality of the spirits she had drunk.'

You have been warned.

IRONY

Noted Scots explorer James Bruce risked life and limb to venture into the most remote and dangerous corners of Africa during the 1760s and 1770s. His stories of the interior of the Dark Continent were so dramatic that he was accused of writing fiction. After all this adventuring, however, he died at the family home in Stirlingshire in 1794 following a dinner party, when he fell down stairs hurrying to escort an old lady to her carriage.

JOBS

Dealing with death offers a variety of job opportunities from the modern, highly mechanised gravedigger to preacher and from mortuary attendant to crematorium technician. The range of skills required by the latter help to give us an idea of the sensitive nature of this work. According to the Learndirect web site, the crematorium technician is required to spend most of their time indoors, with long periods spent standing up. In terms of skills, these range from bereavement care to horticulture and the most relevant are:

† A great deal of tact and discretion
† Ability to deal with grieving people with sympathy and respect
† Good communications skills for liaising with ministers, mourners and undertakers
† Good administration and record-keeping skills
† Ability to pay attention to detail and work within set regulations for burial
† Some knowledge of gardening is helpful

JOKES AND JESTERS

David Barclay, beadle and gravedigger at East Anster in Fife in the early 1800s, was a man who took his job very seriously. At the time of the Burke and Hare atrocities in Edinburgh, a couple of students thought they would up brighten up the holiday by playing a prank on Davie. Knocking on his door, just as he was about to head for bed, the young bucks, after no end of mysterious hints, put some coins in the gravedigger's mitt, saying, 'Now will you help us lift the young widow buried two days ago?'

The old man started back and shouted on his daughter, 'Kirsty, bring my stick, quick, quick, quick – there'll never be a livin' sowl ta'en out o' Anster kirkyard in my time, ye villains!'

Exit chastened students pursued by stick-wielding beadle.

Alan Spence's marvellous novel about the undertaking business in Glasgow, *Way to Go*, delightfully highlights the paradoxical world of the people who make a living from the dead. Early in the book, the young hero asks the hearse driver about the nature of heaven and hell. No philosophical answers are forthcoming but he does offer this wee gem of a joke:

> Saint Peter's feeling tired one day, so Christ comes along and offers to take over for a bit, give him a wee break. Fine says Peter, and away he goes, leaving him to it. So Christ's sitting there, and after a while this old boy comes doddering up to the gates, asks if he can get in. Well Christ goes through the procedure like, asks him about his life. And the more the old boy tells him, the more interested Christ gets.

I grew up in a small town, he says, I was a carpenter.

Oh aye, says Christ.

I had only one son, and I wanted him to follow me into the business.

Uh huh?

But God had other plans for him. My son left home and went out into the world.

Aye?

He became very famous.

And by this time Christ is so excited, he can't keep it in any longer.

He shouts out Father!

And the old boy looks at him, and says Pinocchio!

JUDGEMENT DAY

In 'The Lay of the Last Minstrel', written in the early 1800s, Sir Walter Scott sounded a wake-up call to those who might dismiss Judgement Day as a Biblical fiction:

> That day of wrath, that dreadful day,
> When heaven and earth shall pass away,
> What power shall be the sinner's stay?
> How shall he meet that dreadful day?

Oddly the Bible, which normally scares the pants off you in relation to post-mortem matters, has some beautiful, inspiring, interesting things to say about the day of judgement. Perhaps the most famous reference is in First Corinthians and it is one that features so often at Scottish funerals:

Behold I show you a mystery. We shall not all sleep, but we shall all be changed. In a moment, in the twinkling of an eye, at the last trump: for the trumpet shall sound, and the dead shall be raised incorruptible, and we shall be changed . . . Death is swallowed up in victory. O death, where is they sting? O, grave where is thy victory?

South Uist already has a legend of the dreadful day when the grave-yards gave up their dead. This strange preliminary to Judgement Day saw the dead rise from every kirkyard for a 'day out' roaming the island like so many extras from Michael Jackson's 'Thriller' video. Seems the newly-buried looked much as they had done in life and were recognised. But those who had been below surface for a wee while were apparently and unsurprisingly maggot-eaten, gross, fairly odiferous and 'horrible beyond words', according to local writer Otta Swire. The people took to the sea, the only place they felt safe from this unholy crew, and it was the crowing of a cock, from a croft roof, which eventually sent the zombies stumbling back to their lairs. This tale may also help to explain the unusually elevated social status of the cockerel in the Uists.

South Uist in particular, according to Swire, seems a place of many stories of the dead who will not stay put. These tales usually only concern the few days between death and burial and one wonders if at least one or two instances may not have been due to people coming out of comas and terrifying attendants and mourners.

JUSTICE

As late as the end of the seventeenth century, a strange procedure was used to determine the guilt of a murderer. Suspects were called to approach the body of the victim on its funeral bier. If fresh blood appeared, this was taken as a token of the person's guilt. This was generally termed the Bier-Rite Trial.

KEEPSAKES

Queen Victoria took so many reminders of the life she left behind with her that she could scarcely fit in her coffin. The contents included Prince Albert's dressing gown, a plaster cast of her hand, numerous photographs, several pieces of jewellery and some shawls and handkerchiefs. From a Scottish perspective, the most interesting fact is that the queen instructed that a lock of hair and a photograph of her devoted attendant, ghillie and friend John Brown should be placed in her left hand.

KISTING

This was the act of laying the body in the coffin. The Reformed Church did not see this as being a religious event but gradually ministers began to attend kistings and kisting took on the character of a brief service. This procedure was reported in rural parts of Scotland right into the middle of the twentieth century.

LAIRS

A lair can be a resting place for animals or a bed but, for our purposes, the most common Scottish usage relates to a burial place or grave. It is generally a burial space purchased by a family or individual in a graveyard. Many folk still believe that, when they buy a lair, they actually buy the ground. Unfortunately, it is only the right of burial that is sold.

A guaranteed last resting place to await Judgement Day was seen as essential. In Glasgow in 1594, kirk officers were having to deal with a spate of incidents where the dead were being buried clandestinely in other people's lairs due to shortage of consecrated ground.

LAST CALL

Undertakers confirm that something like 65 per cent of families still visit the body of the deceased in the funeral parlour, although very few keep the deceased at home.

LAST SUPPER

In rural Scotland, the tradition was that once the corpse had been 'stretched' on a board and clothed in a coarse linen wrapper, a wooden plate containing salt and earth, unmixed apparently, was laid on the breast of the deceased. It is also recorded that cheese and sometimes a slab of turf were laid on the dear departed. Generally all fires were extinguished in the room where the corpse was laid.

The story is told of Alexander MacDougall, an octogenarian Highlander who finally gave way under the pressure of years. As he lay dying, the rich aroma of freshly baked shortbread reached his deathbed. With one last gallant effort, the old man hauled himself ben the hoose to the kitchen where, with his withered old hand, he reached for a glorious, golden slice. At that precise moment, a wooden spoon rapped his knuckles and his dear wife declared, 'Get yer hauns aff of that, ye auld bugger, they're fur the wake.'

LAST WISHES

Don't let the awkward squad fire over me.
                    Robert Burns, shortly before his death in 1796

LAST WORDS

In my end is my beginning.
                    Mary Queen of Scots (1542-87)

Anne Gordon, in her admirable book *Death is for the Living*, catalogues a whole series of bizarre exchanges between the nearly-deceased and the folk they are about to leave behind. She records the instance of a dying Aberdeenshire man discussing with his son on what day the funeral should be held and agreeing to avoid the day of the Huntly market.

> Toodle-oo!!
> Beat Generation poet Allan Ginsberg's last words, as disclosed at
> the Edinburgh Book Festival in 2001

We often read of people on their last legs dishing out the orders to their nearest and dearest, even in relation to the funeral arrangements. On one occasion, an old boy, who had loved his dram, gave detailed instructions to his son to ensure that everyone got a whisky at the wake. Says the auld yin, 'As I'll no' be there mysel', I'll hae mine noo.'

Similarly, the story is told of the old woman who, as a last request, asked her husband to travel in the same coach as her mother in an attempt to end a long-running feud. His reply, 'Ah'll do it tae please ye but it'll completely spoil the day for me.'

LAUGHTER

When you look carefully at the turbulent times of Sir Thomas Urquhart of Cromarty (1611–1660), he didn't really have a lot to laugh about. Yet this intriguing man, who studied at King's College, Aberdeen, before travelling in France, Spain and Italy, is known to history as a poet, historian and, more significantly, as one of the century's most notable humorists.

The period through which he lived was characterised by strife – what with the National Covenant and the Cromwellian occupation. Covenanters and bishops' men tore at each other's throats with a passion that only such a civil/religious struggle seems capable of arousing. They were serious and troubled times indeed and Urquhart nailed his colours firmly to the royalist mast.

Captured at the Battle of Worcester and imprisoned in the Tower of London, he was still allowed a remarkable freedom and completed several works including *The Pedigree*, an account of how the Urquhart family could be traced back to Adam via the Queen of Sheba. However, Sir Thomas earns his place in the pantheon of odd endings because of his reaction to the Restoration of Charles II in 1660. While the streets of Edinburgh ran with claret, fireworks burst overhead and cannon roared out in salute, Urquhart, living abroad again, is said to have died during a joyous fit of laughter at the news.

LAYING THE CHIEF TO REST

As we find elsewhere, journeys of twenty, thirty, or even one hundred miles were common in the Highlands in order that the deceased might be laid to rest in the graves of their forefathers. Emigration aside, no matter how far they'd strayed from home, the ambition was to spend eternity wi' their ain folk. Without roads, the coffin was shouldered over these distances in remarkably quick time. Rivers were forded, bogs crossed and storms braved to get to the wee corner of a distant kirkyard where a grave was waiting to be filled.

In the Highlands, it came to be looked upon as a sort of disgrace to be taken to the churchyard in a hearse. When the last Glengarry died in 1828, it was suggested sending a hearse from Inverness but clansmen reacted furiously, saying the hearse would never be allowed to enter the glen. It was clear that only by the hands and sturdy shoulders of the people would the chief be carried to his grave. They pledged to a man that Mac-Mhic-Alastair would never be carried to Kilfinnan in a cart. We have a fascinating anonymous eye-witness account of the funeral of that last chief of Glengarry, Colonel McDonnell:

> At daybreak columns of the clan streamed down from every glen, each body being headed by the pipes. They arrived at the castle lining up on the lawn in their various companies and in the large open space before the door was pitched the great yellow banner of the clan surmounted by a spreading bush of heather, the badge of Clan Donald. Shortly after the doors swung open and in the gloomy hall beyond appeared the coffin with four stalwart Highlanders bearing flaming torches at each corner.
>
> Waxen tapers fixed between the antlers upon the whitened stags' skulls that surrounded the hall cast a weird light upon the tartans and armour covering the walls.
>
> The 'ceann-tigh' or heads of the cadet families were already assembled and as they lifted the coffin Glengarry's piper who had taken his stand beside the colours, blew up the march 'cille-chriost'.
>
> It was a terribly wild day and a thunderstorm was raging as the procession moved off. Passing the barbican of the old ruined castle a brilliant flash of lightning lit up the sky followed by a crash of thunder. As the roar of thunder rolled round the hills, Allan Dall, the old blind bard of the Chief burst forth in a piteous wail. Then waving his bonnet towards the sky he broke into a wild lament,

calling the heavens and the storm to the grave of his Chief.

In a few moments the Gaelic refrain was taken up by all present, and a deep surge from two thousand voices rolled forth the chorus to the skies.

Is, sona 'Bhean-bains' air an éirich grian,
Is beannaicht 'an corp air an tuit an fhras'.

Happy the bride that the sun shines on,
Blessed the corpse that the rain rains upon.

By the time the procession reached the graveyard at Kilfinnan, the stream was swollen to a roaring torrent: there was no bridge across the burn as there is today. But the Highlanders, well used to fording streams on such occasions, plunged fearlessly into the flood. When the coffin reached mid-stream, it seemed for a moment as if the bearers with their charge would be swept away. Then Angus the Chief's eldest son flung out the war-cry from the other side:

Lamh dhearg bhuadhach chlann dhomhuill!

Those behind pressed eagerly forward and the bier, borne by the strong arms of the willing clansmen safely won the further bank. A few minutes later the last Chief of Glengarry lay side by side with his famous ancestor 'Black John' of Killiecrankie, beneath the green sod of that little plot of ground, all that now remains to link his family with the glens and the people he loved so well.

LETTERS

In centuries past, unsurprisingly, there was a great deal of formality attached to funeral correspondence. Below is the text of a brief communication received in March 1780 by Mr William Shortridge, partner in a Vale of Leven printfield, and written by the recently bereaved minister at Dumbarton. The letter, I think, is a strange contrast between what appears to be genuine affection and quite open obsequiousness:

> Dr. Sir – It pleased the Wise and Righteous Sovereign to remove from me on Wednesday last by death the Desire of my Eyes – her Precious Remains are to be buried here tomorrow at 4 o'clock. If it is at all convenient for you to attend, your company there will much oblige,
>
> Dr. Sir, your most hum'le servt, Jas. Oliphant

LIFEBLOOD

What, think you, are the most notable bloodstains to seep through the gory pages of Scottish history and romance? Perhaps you'd find a strong lobby for the 'damned spot' that had Lady Macbeth reaching for the Swarfega? Or the sanguinary stain on the floor of the anteroom in the Palace of Holyroodhouse where David Rizzio, the musician boyfriend of Mary, Queen of Scots, was severely ventilated by a group of dour, knife-wielding Scots nobles? I've always been slightly confused that palace guides and officials don't make more of the fact that this particular stain appears to have been miraculously re-vitalised at the start of each tourist season. Have we

Glamis Castle

as a nation overlooked a minor miracle – a mysterious unexplained phenomenon right on our own doorstep?

Both of these blemishes would be leading contenders in our search but surely the runaway winner has to be the mark on the floor of King Malcolm's room at Glamis Castle. Here, in 1034, Malcolm II, who had annoyed his contemporaries by breaking the Pictish system of inheritance by nominating his grandson, Duncan, as his successor, was cut down by a gang of rebels. The murder, having been committed at such a mist-shrouded date, is not chronicled in great detail but we are told that the king was hacked to pieces with claymores and that, remarkably, every drop of his blood oozed into the floorboards. Malcolm's killers, however, did not survive to boast of the assassination. As they fled across a frozen loch, the ice gave way under them and they were drowned.

The fact that the floorboards seem to have been replaced at least once since that time and that the castle is inevitably much-changed does not deter those who value such a gory anecdote. What is certain is that this murder opened the castle's casebook as a thriving centre for ghosts and ghoulies. It is unquestionably Scotland's most haunted building and, even on a bright summer's day, carries an eerie aspect.

LITTLE ARROWS

Flint arrowheads are found widely throughout Scotland. These relics of our hunter-gatherer ancestors are also known as elf-shots because they were thought to have been fired by the fairy people at mortals. They always proved fatal even though the skin strangely – you might say conveniently – never showed any abrasion. Sewing the arrowhead into the lapel of a jacket offered immunity from further attack.

LOGIC

Do troubled spirits of the long- and the not-so-long-dead remain around us, inhabiting a shadow world by our side, their appearances triggered by emotion locked in buildings and furniture and perhaps in other people? In brief, do ghosts exist? James Boswell, the companion of Dr Samuel Johnson, records in his *Life of Johnson*:

> It is wonderful that five thousand years have now elapsed since the creation of the world, and still it is undecided whether or not there has ever been an instance of the spirit of any person appearing after death. All argument is against it; but all belief is for it.

LYCHGATES

These are small porches at the church gates. They are characteristically English, having a redolence of villages in the rolling Cotswolds. Nevertheless, there are some interesting examples in Scotland.

Not far from my former home in Aberdeenshire, at the peaceful wee community of Chapel of Garioch, is a lychgate built in the early 1600s and described by Anne Gordon as a funeral porch. Another picturesque example can be found at the parish church of Luss on Loch Lomondside.

In Pre-Reformation days, the lychgate was where the coffin was laid during the first part of the funeral service before it was taken into the church – a ritual that symbolised the passing from life to death. Later, lychgates became merely resting places where the coffin-bearers were relieved of their load as they waited for the minister to arrive – very handy if it was raining, especially if the minister wasn't the best of time-keepers.

MALE CHAUVINISM

An odd tale is told of the old churchyard of Kingarth on the island of Bute. The burying ground is constructed on two levels. According to tradition the upper section was composed of consecrated earth brought from Rome. The story is that local women who refused to assist St Blane in bringing up the earth from the ships on which it had been imported – or perhaps they carelessly lost some along the way – were told that, as a result, neither they nor any of their sex would be allowed to be buried in the sacred mould. This order was carefully observed. The belief was that, if they did inter females on the upper ground, such bodies would surely rise to the surface. This strange practice was not laid aside until 1661.

MANY HAPPY RETURNS

There was a Lochaber man who, although an invalid, would shuffle out of the house every evening with his hat on and his plaid over his shoulder and sit at the end of the house, hands leaning on the top of his staff. He and his wife were childless but their nephew stayed with

A Highland croft

them. After the old man's death the boy decided he would play a prank on his aunt by rigging himself up in his uncle's hat and plaid and sitting at the end of the house. As the woman came along the path in the gloaming, she called out confidently, 'You're there then!' Without waiting for a response she pressed on into the house.

On the second evening, she halted and offered a verbal barrage to the 'spectre' at the end of the house, 'You're there again then? Most likely they did not put you deep enough at Kilmallie. If you take it on you to come here a third time, I will lift you out of Kilmallie myself and put you in the Minister's Pool; and see if you rise out of that!'

MEDIUM RARE

In 1570, Gilbert, Earl of Cassilis, the self-styled King of Carrick in Ayrshire, partially roasted a man called William Stewart over a spit in an attempt to extort cash.

MILITARY SERVICE

FROM THE TOUCH-LINE TO THE TRENCHES
Scores of Scottish professional footballers, many of them household names, signed up in 1914 for war service. Among the clubs most severely touched were Hearts who lost half of their senior squad in the Battle of the Somme.

MINING

In the event of a fatal accident in the Fife coalfields, every collier 'within knowledge of that accident' would, without bidding, come to the surface.

MINISTER (HEADLESS)

At Logiealmond in Perthshire a headless minister was reputed to haunt the Moor of Shannoch and the Craggan Wood. He carried a large bible on his back, knapsack-style, and when heard preaching his theme was 'Oh, this is sinfu' land'. Great story but, pray, without a head, from which part of his anatomy did he speak?

MISSING IN ACTION

The Hay family, the hereditary Earls of Errol, lost the Fourth Earl at the Battle of Flodden. The family burial table at Cupar Abbey shows a blank with reference to the burial place of this particular nobleman. This is generally taken to mean that his body was never brought from the battlefield. The Earl's brother Thomas and eighty-seven members of the Hay family fell at Flodden with their chief.

MISTAKEN IDENTITY

Death comes to us all – it's a fact. But, occasionally, it is prematurely trumpeted causing nothing but confusion. It was the American writer Mark Twain who famously announced, 'Reports of my death are greatly exaggerated.'

However, in the early 1900s William 'Skatehorn' Laughton, a noted Orcadian eccentric, went one better. After reading a report of death in the local paper, he earnestly declared, 'I saw the report – but I did not believe it.'

It was also in Orkney that a missing fisherman, having swum for hours to reach the shore, was greeted by a crofter with the immortal words, 'Were you the man who droon'd this efternoon?'

MISTIMING

The Grim Reaper, on occasion, strikes at the most inopportune times but occasionally we don't help ourselves. The tragic story is told of the man found dead on rail tracks in the West End of Glasgow, obviously having been struck by a train the previous night. Police were convinced that he was probably in the process of removing copper wire. The operation seems to have been carefully planned but his misfortune was explained when an out-of-date railway timetable was found in his pocket.

MOCK FUNERALS

In the 1980s, an eighty-seven-year-old Italian man, 'dying to see what his funeral would be like', organised a mock event in the town of Poggio Nativo. The event included a procession from his church to the cemetery, complete with the town band playing solemn music. Alexandro Polverari, a retired local government official, wore a three-piece black suit and hat and walked at the head of a procession which was comprised of a band, family members and a column of almost 200 cars.

MORTALITY

In Ancient Egypt, after any major booze-up or festivity, a mummy was wheeled into the banqueting hall to remind the carousing guests of their mortality – eat, drink and merry because tomorrow you might be food for the crows, etc. After putting an appropriate damper on the proceedings and sobering up the revellers, the mummy was wheeled out again, no doubt shouting, 'And, by the way, yer tea's oan the table.'

MORTCLOTH

This was a large cloth – black velvet was the business by the 1700s – which was used to cover the coffin prior to burial or, in harder times, to cover the shroud when a coffin was too great an expense. It could be owned by burghs, parishes, craft guilds or even individuals. Even into the 1800s, not every parish could afford an elaborate burial cloth and so the richer parishes would hire them out. This often providing an important source of revenue. The Kirk Session at Invera'an in Strathspey got their cloth in 1750 and agreed to hire it out. In the lower end of the parish, the cost was a shilling. At Glenlivet, it was eighteen pence and, in any other parish, the fee was two shillings. The theory was that the further the cloth had to travel the more it might be damaged 'by being carried to those remote places'.

The mortcloth could have a very strange effect on people. A laird of Aldbar, near Brechin, was to be married to the daughter of a neighbouring proprietor. The woman decided, as a token of remembrance, that she would gift a mortcloth to her local parish. She ordered both the cloth and her wedding dress from the same firm in Edinburgh. As a result of a misunderstanding both items ended up at Aldbar where the laird, said to be a man of nervous disposition, opened the parcel, read it as an omen and hurried off to Montrose where he drowned himself. The bride died soon after and the mortcloth was first used at her own funeral. Sorry, we seem to have dropped into a cheerless mode yet again.

Like the charge for the use of the church bell at funerals (*See* **Bells**), the hire of the mortcloth could often be a source of controversy. To try to get around mortcloth dues, people often used a hearse without a cloth, thereby defrauding the poor of the parish who benefited from the mortcloth money.

In Aberdour, in Fife, there was a 'small civil war' about mortcloth tariffs in 1650. As a means of bringing down the charges, tailors in the community arranged for an 'opposition' mortcloth to be sewn. Tough negotiations eventually saw the kirk session take possession of the tailors' mortcloth. Parishioners, undaunted then arranged to hire a cloth from a neighbouring parish before, in a final, dramatic move, the kirk session ended the dispute by declaring that no grave would be dug until an assurance had been given that the parish mortcloth would be used.

MORTSAFES

See **Bodysnatchers**

MOTORING

It is said with an alarming degree of accuracy that, in Scotland's cities, there are really only two types of pedestrian – the quick and the dead.

MOURNING

The more remote the Scottish location, it seems, the more primitive and intense was the mourning. The seventeenth-century traveller Martin Martin, on a visit to St Kilda, reported that, on the death of the laird, the people had left their homes for two days to mourn him in the fields. According to Anne Gordon, they did so 'in a manner that was positively Biblical'.

MUMMIFICATION

Asked to name the world's most famous mummy, most folk would surely plump for the Egyptian boy king Tutankhamun whose fabulous grave was uncovered during the early twentieth century. However, a Scots descendant in the American West has a claim to this unlikely title.

Elmer J McCurdy had more adventures after his death than most of us have during our lifetime. McCurdy, a train robber, was killed by a posse in Oklahoma in 1911. A local undertaker embalmed the body and put it on display at a nickel a peek. In 1916, two men arrived on the scene posing as McCurdy's brothers and reclaimed the corpse. For decades, they exhibited Elmer's remains all across the

United States as a fairground attraction, keeping the old boy spruced up with lacquer and paint. Disrespectful visitors used to stuff used carnival tickets in his mouth.

The mummy of Elmer McCurdy finally came to rest in a fun house in Long Beach, California – until a crew showed up to film an episode of the *Six Million Dollar Man*. The mummy had been taken for a stage dummy until one of McCurdy's arms broke off, after being struck by a stage light. The accident revealed human bone. Police inquiries uncovered his identity and his body was returned to Oklahoma for burial.

To give Scotland a further boost in the mummy stakes, it is worth recording that two embalmed individuals were discovered under the floor of the Bronze Age site at Cladh Hallan in South Uist in 2003. The discovery of the man and woman, older than Tutankhamun, not only indicates that the early inhabitants of Scotland mummified some of their nobility or priests but it also makes them the oldest mummies discovered anywhere in Europe. Experts believe the bodies had been bound tightly in leather or cloth which had disintegrated in the wet Hebridean conditions. To help preserve the bodies, experts believe they were wind-dried, pickled, smoked over a peat fire or dipped in a peat bog. Neat, eh?

MYSTERIES

Events surrounding the strange death of the Fifth Earl of Huntly, in May 1576 at Strathbogie Castle, and its odd sequel remain a compelling mystery of the sixteenth century. The earl apparently fell down in a fit while playing a Saturday afternoon game of football. He foamed at the mouth and nostrils, struggled with his hands, stared wildly, vomited blood and expired four hours later. He was laid out in state in one of the larger rooms in the castle. Candles were lit around the body and preparations began for the funeral.

The following morning, mourners had gathered in a room adjacent to the one housing the corpse when one man, while explaining how much he owed to the late earl, 'fell flat down on his face to the ground'. At first, the company were convinced that he was dead but windows were flung open and, after lying in a fever for a time, he fully recovered. Next day, a senior member of the household, John Hamilton, was taken ill in an identical way, collapsing and moaning that he was very cold and sick. Again he recovered.

An Aberdeen surgeon had been called to 'bowel' the corpse of the earl, which was then removed to the chapel. Four days after the death, events took an even stranger turn. From behind the door where the corpse had lain, the earl's brother Patrick Gordon heard 'a great noise or din'. Gordon called on John Hamilton to investigate but he refused the solo mission and they eventually entered the room together. It was dusk and, though the odd noises continued, they could see nothing. For more than an hour, the sounds went on and others were called to witness the odd phenomenon. According to James Bannatyne, secretary to John Knox, who relates this weird tale, those at Strathbogie were sworn to secrecy lest it be thought that the earl had risen from the dead.

Whether poisoning – deliberate or accidental – was to blame, as some think, it was not the first bizarre occurrence involving the corpse of a Huntly earl. In 1563, the Crown was so anxious to bring the House of Huntly to justice for their rebellious behaviour in the north that the embalmed body of the fourth earl, George Gordon, was cairted to Edinburgh for sentence – four months after his death at the Battle of Corrichie.

Names

My nomination for the cheeriest place in Scotland just has to be Castle Campbell near Dollar in Clackmannanshire. Otherwise known as Castle Gloom, it stands on a rocky outcrop between the burns of Care and Sorrow. If the residents of the castle had been the De'Ath family, it would have been no surprise,

All tombstones tell a story but the search goes on for the location of the graves of the following colourful occupants:

Otta B Alive
Kerry M Orff
U R Gone
Ted N Buried
Yetta Nother

And somewhere out there is a tombstone which carries a name that has a sobering message for us all:

Yul B Next

In superstitious fishing communities, it was frowned on to mention the name of the recently deceased and instead circumlocution in the style of 'Him that has gane' was used.

In certain parts of Scotland, particularly the north, until the body was placed therein, the coffin was generally known as the kist.

NECROPHILIA

An unhealthy sexual interest in the deceased as in 'I used to be into necrophilia – but then they closed down the Locarno.' (for middle-aged Glaswegian males only).

> The grave's a fine and private place
> But none, I think, do there embrace.
>
> 'To His Coy Mistress'
> Andrew Marvell (1621–78)

NECROPHOBIA

The dictionary defines this as a morbid fear of death – yeah, like there are lots of other kinds of fear of death!

NEW MINISTERS AND PRIESTS

Sociologists will tell you that bereavement counsellors and psychiatrists are becoming the new 'ritual specialists' of our era. Colin Parkes suggests that the fundamental difference in the approach is that the minister has traditionally seen death as a transition for the dead whereas this new breed conceives of death as a transition for the bereaved.

Sorn Parish Church, winner of the Cemetery of the Year award for 2003

NICE PLACE TO SPEND ETERNITY

Scotland is particularly well blessed in beautiful graveyard locations. After exhaustive research and consultation, I offer below some spectacular Scottish settings to spend the time 'twixt now and Judgement Day. The thought of spending eternity in one spot must be scary for folk who are constantly chasing their tails in this age of easy mobility. But making a selection for eternity in advance is maybe something worth considering – if only to ease the stress on the poor old relatives. Here is my strictly personal choice:

† St Boniface Kirkyard, Papa Westray, Orkney – hingin' on the edge of eternity
† Glasgow Necropolis – truly a creepy Victorian city of the dead
† St Nicholas Churchyard, Aberdeen – an urban boneyard busy with passers-by
† Balquhidder Kirkyard – Rob Roy lies here amid a fantastic mountain setting
† Largs Cemetery, North Ayrshire – a contemporary design offering tranquillity
† Rothes and Mortlach Cemeteries, Moray – adjacent to distilleries
† Calton Burial Ground, Edinburgh – join David Hume for an overview of Scottish history
† St Monans Churchyard, Fife – looking out across the wide Forth
† Kirk Alloway, Ayrshire – 'Weel done Cutty Sark!'
† Greyfriars Kirkyard, Edinburgh – a great view, loads of history, plenty of wraiths and Wee Boaby too! Awwwwww

Glasgow Necropolis

Obesity

Here's a timely warning for the overweight Scot. If, on shuffling off the mortal coil, you don't want to become a pollution threat then lose some of that beef! Recently, crematorium superintendents in the Midlands received an instruction not to burn fat bodies in the afternoon – apparently they create too much ash. The unlikely explanation is that large bodies burn too quickly when the ovens have been working all day. The order asked the crematorium bosses to weigh the bodies prior to cremation and adjust the burning schedule to keep the problem under control.

In another sad episode, we discovered this year that there is no crematorium in Scotland that can handle a corpse weighing 30-plus stone.

Obituaries

Now, here's a tip from my days in the Scottish newspaper business. If you want to make a splash with your obituary in the big two – *The Herald* and *The Scotsman* – then the best day to die on is a Saturday.

Both newspapers carry extensive 'morgues', previously-prepared obituaries. But, with the whole of Sunday to put the obituary together, a great deal of extra work can be done in terms of tributes to expand the obituary and possibly even supply quotes suitable for use in an accompanying news story, if you really are or think yourself a bit of a celeb. But a word of warning – before you set out to get yourself into the death slot, a lot has changed in the obituary business in recent years. In days gone by, misdemeanours went unrecorded and obituaries were sycophantic praise poems. Back then, coy phrases such as 'he never married' would have given a discreet clue to a person's homosexual background. But such practices are long gone. Increasingly, obituary writers tell it like it is or, more accurately, like it was. So beware – you are now liable to be portrayed warts and all.

And here's another tip. The more eccentric your behaviour, even if in truth you are a bit of a non-entity, then the bigger your chance of getting a mention. In years past, Melvin Buckhart would never have made the obituary columns but, in 2001, *The Daily Telegraph* paid tribute to the man who was a sideshow performer famed for his ability to drive a six-inch nail into his head without flinching!

As the 'Review' section of *The Observer* noted a couple of years ago:

> One-legged inventors, lepidopterist wrestlers, tax-fiddling cardinals
> . . . readers who forget to read the broadsheets' obits pages are
> missing out on much of life.

Well, then, are you happy enough to leave your obituary to acquaintances who might use the opportunity to settle old scores, when you are no longer around to dig them up about it? Web sites, as you might expect, offer all sorts of advice on this topic. However, a Scottish spin is needed. Here is a suggested structure for a do-it-yourself obituary.

Announcement

McGurk, Wee Tam, died 12 August 2008 while doon the corner shop for fags.

Biographical Information:
Born in Govan in 1948 where he spent most of his life. Once travelled to Rutherglen but found the language difficult to understand. With his big brother 'Silencer' McGurk, he founded Copland Road Exhausts and coined the slogan 'McGurk's, A Breath of Fresh Air in the Exhaust Business'.

Survivor Information:
Apart from his brother, Tam is survived by his wife Persephone and children Britney and Bertie.

Scheduled Ceremonies and Gatherings of Remembrance:
Tam will be laid to rest next week in Pollok Estate, beneath an old oak, in a woodland burial, as he wished. Blue nose to the core, Tam threatened to come back and haunt anyone who described it as a green burial. Friends and anyone who was due a pint from the wee man should meet up in The Scabby Cuddy on Tuesday night for a celebration of Tam's life but, more importantly, also to decide who takes his place in the pool team.

Contributions or Flowers:
No flowers please. All donations should be made to The Carntyne Home for Retired Racing Greyhounds.

Now, that sort of approach is more or less guaranteed to win you a corner in the local rag.

OLD FOLK

Psychiatrists studying the preoccupations of the very old at nursing homes throughout Scotland discovered that a surprising proportion had Henry F Lyte's classic funeral ditty 'Abide with Me' running around in their heads. Described as a hymn of comfort, it just pipped 'Another One Bites the Dust' as the oldies' favourite.

Old Mortality

One of the most striking characters of Scottish fiction is Old Mortality. Created by Sir Walter Scott, he is an old man who keeps the faith alive by restoring the graves and monuments of his fellow Covenanters. Scott based the character on stonecutter Robert Paterson (1658–1719). An adherent of the strict Cameronian sect, Paterson was born near Hawick and he spent forty years on this mission of remembrance.

Omens

There were many, many omens of misfortune to be found in the flora and fauna of the Western Highlands. If, for example, you saw a foal with his back to you, if you heard a cuckoo before having your tea, spotted a snipe sitting on top of tuft of grass or noticed a snail on a bare ledge then these were all harbingers bad news. If, by any chance, you happen to witness all four of these events simultaneously then you might as well get your box ordered up. The Grim Reaper has your card marked.

> When Dee and Don shall run in one
> And Tweed shall run in Tay,
> And the bonnie water o' Urie
> Shall bear the Bass away.

Attributed to Thomas the Rhymer, these four lines refer to a medieval motte-and-bailey mound, the foundations for a timber-frame castle, at the kirkyard on the outskirts of Inverurie. The castle dwellers are said to have been infected with plague and interred in the mound. A local belief held that, if the Urie flooded (which, from my own recollection, it does every year) and took the mound away, the plague would be released again so barriers were raised to protect the site.

In the 1660s, the Third Earl of Balcarres formed an attachment through the Court with the splendidly titled Mademoiselle Mauritia de Nassau, a daughter of the Count of Beverwaert in Holland. On the day of their wedding, the company had assembled but the bridegroom had forgotten all about the arrangement. When reminded it was his big day, he raced off, forgetting the ring. He borrowed one from a friend but forgot to check its suitability. It was, unfortunately, a mourning ring embossed with a skull and cross-bones. When the bride saw this, she fainted and, on recovering, declared that she would die within a year. Right enough, twelve months later she died in childbirth.

Another odd, and very specific, omen of impending death was the sighting of a rainbow that was contained within the stone or turf boundaries of a Highland township.

ONE-THOUSAND-AND-ONE USES FOR FLAT GRAVESTONES (ALMOST)

1. For signing religious documents such as the National Covenant
2. For a picnic table when visiting the ancestors
3. For getting a better view of the wedding party leaving the kirk
4. For a shove ha'penny arena with a surface like Hampden Park
5. For a splendid seat while you are contemplating your origins

Optimism

A great number of lives were lost among Scottish emigrants during the great exodus to North America in the eighteenth and nineteenth centuries. The expats died of sickness and, sometimes, of despair. That the voyagers had little idea of the great danger to life and rigours ahead of them on departure is well illustrated by the story of a group of Lochaber emigrants leaving in 1802. As they were sailing down Loch Linnhe, a woman from the Grant contingent was anxious to know if they were passed Corran Ferry which lies some nine miles south of Fort William and is notorious for strong cross currents. Told that they were passing well away from the problem area, the woman heaved a sigh of relief and the innocent soul declared that 'now that they were past Corran, they we're o'er the worst of the journey'. Nine weeks of hardship, fear and misery lay ahead before Canada was reached.

Every exit is an entrance to somewhere else

Anon.

Ostracism

The bringer of death – the public executioner – was always set apart from his fellow human beings. In Edinburgh during the 1700s, the public hangman always had a pew to himself in the Tolbooth Church and, at the regular communion services, the clergyman was obliged to serve a separate table for the hangman after the rest of the congregation had left.

Oxymoron

This figure of speech which presents, according to the Oxford Dictionary, a 'pointed conjunction of seeming contradictories' also must be in the running as death's favourite. Some examples:

† Living dead
† Morbid humour
† Bad health
† Mercy killing
† Benign tumour
† Half dead
† Fatally injured
† Born dead
† Buried alive
† Dying is a part of life
† Cheerful undertaker
† Dead livestock
† Clean kill

Oyez! Oyez!

What exactly might we have expected to hear in Scotland in the 1500s as the bellringer tramped the streets to announce a death? From the town records of Edinburgh, we have this example:

Beloved brethren and sisters, I let you to wit that there is ane faithful brother lately departed out of this present world, at the pleesure of Almighty God. His name is Wully Woodcock, third son to Jemmy Woodcock, a cordiner. He lies at the sixt door within the Norgate, close on the Nether Wynd, and I would you gang to his burying on Thursday before twa o'clock.

Packing Them In

In the 1880s, a west coast Highland town is said to have announced the cheering news that tourists had been waiting for:

Visitors to the town are respectfully informed that an excellent and commodious hearse has recently been provided by the local authorities.

Commodious? Excellent! Whit are we waiting for? Pit doon that bucket and spade – this is the chance of a lifetime!

Parting of the Ways

To Earth – the Body,
To Heaven – the Soul,
To Friends – the Memory.

Anon.

After his death in 1873, the heart and entrails of David Livingstone were buried in Zambia while the rest of his body was sent back to London to be interred in Westminster Abbey.

PARTY POOPERS

Of course, there are lots of folk who shiver at the thought of the fuss surrounding funerals – whether burials or cremations – and hope to depart unnoticed, untrumpeted, discreetly. I feel a bit like that myself . . . I rather fancy the idea of vanishing up the Orinoco while on an expedition in the search of a lost city or being vaporised at sixty miles by an incoming comet while attempting the highest ever balloon flight or simply vanishing while on a mission to secure a black pudding supper at the chippie on the corner.

This, of course, is the ultimate selfishness. Those left behind have no tangible evidence of the departed and mourning, at best, can only be partial. However, in *The Catcher in the Rye*, American author J D Salinger caught the mood of those of us who would like to depart stage left, quietly:

> Boy, when you're dead, they really fix you up. I hope to hell when I do die somebody has sense enough to just dump me in the river or something. Anything except sticking me in a goddam cemetery. People coming in and putting a bunch of flowers on your stomach on a Sunday and all that crap. Who wants flowers when you're dead? Nobody.

PASTURE

Some of the richest, best-fertilised soil and sweetest grass is, quite naturally, to be found in Scotland's old burying grounds. Beasts would think themselves in grazing heaven when they found their way amongst the tombstones. However, having their relatives dumped upon by a pig, horse, cow or goat did tend to offend the townsfolk. In 1599 in Paisley, a heavy fine was promised to anyone who let 'whatever horse, ky, or other besteel be apprehended in the kirkyard.

PATIENCE

And come he slow, or come he fast,
It is but Death who comes at last.

'Marmion'
Sir Walter Scott (1771-1832)

A sign prominently displayed at the entrance to a funeral home reads:

Drive Carefully – We're Happy to Wait

PATRIOTISM

Scots, wha hae wi' Wallace bled,
Scots, wham Bruce has aften led,
Welcome to your gory bed –
Or to victorie.

'Robert Bruce's March to Bannockburn'
Robert Burns (1759–96)

184

PEEK-A-BOO

The rather bizarre American idea that coffins, or caskets as they are more often called on the other side of the Atlantic, should have a pane of glass, a viewing window, through which the features of the deceased can be seen, has never caught on in this country.

PESSIMISM/OPTIMISM

Even the longest day has an end.

PESTILENCE

See **Plague**

PICKLING

American scientist, journalist and politician Benjamin Franklin suggested an experiment for the preservation and, hopefully, the eventual resuscitation of the dead. He wanted to be immersed in a vat of Madeira wine and later brought back to life – 'as flies drowned in Madeira wine' were sometimes capable of being revived. Personally, I wonder about the authenticity of this story because it is reminiscent of the tale of the Scottish distillery worker who drowned in a vat of best malt. Death would have been quicker if he hadn't got out three times to go to the toilet.

Piper's Place

At funerals the piper normally followed the coffin, since his place was always at the head of the deceased, while by contrast at marriages he played at the front of the procession. Often, in the Highlands, two men would walk a few hundred yards in advance of the cortege and offer refreshments in the name of the deceased to anyone they met on the way. This parting cup was intended as a last act of hospitality – always a darling virtue with Highlanders – and carried with it the tacit obligation of offering a prayer for the person who was being carried to the grave.

Plague

In sixteenth-century Scotland, the death sentence was applied to those who visited plague victims either without supervision, outside permitted hours or for concealing the fact that the 'pest' had entered your house. In Edinburgh, plague victims were forced to remove themselves – bag and baggage – to the Burgh-Moor where they were lodged in 'wretched huts' hastily erected for accommodation.

Of course, there's nothing at all romantic about bubonic plague. The outbreak of the second half of the 1640s was brought to Scotland in the baggage of a returning Covenanting army and it killed 20,000 people. Fear was everywhere. Traders boiled coins, plague houses were 'cleansed' with heather smoke and gallows were erected to string up unwanted plague refugees from neighbouring towns. Yet, against this sombre backdrop in Scotland at this time, there emerges one of the most tragic, but tender, plague stories remembered anywhere in Europe – the legend of Bessie Bell and

Mary Gray. These Perthshire girls, daughters of local lairds, were inseparable companions. On hearing news of the first plague victims in nearby Perth, they decided that they would cut themselves off from the outside world and retire to a den which they constructed north of the River Almond, a couple of miles from Methven. A contemporary ballad, of which only a couple of stanzas survive, tells us:

> Bessie Bell and Mary Gray,
> They were two bonnie lassies,
> They biggit a bower on yon burn brae,
> And theekit it oweere wi' rashes.

The actual location of their forest home was said to be on the Lynedoch Estate, which belonged to Mary's father and was at a beautiful spot on the side of the Beanchie Burn. They lived there in seclusion while plague raged through surrounding communities. But, according to folklore, they caught the infection from a young man who was in love with both girls and made regular trips into the woods with their provisions. The girls died in their bower and, as plague victims, they were buried away from the kirkyard – at Dronoch Haugh, beside the Almond.

More than a century later, in 1781, Major Barry, then owner of Lynedoch, recalled how, on first coming to the estate, he was shown a heap of stones almost covered with briars, thorns and ferns which he was assured was the last resting place of Bessie and Mary. The major ordered the rubbish to be removed from this 'little spot of classic ground' and had the ground cleared. He enclosed it with a wall, planted it with shrubs and fixed a stone in the wall recording the girls' names. This grave, in land now owned by the Earl of

Mansfield of Scone Palace, can be seen to this day and is clearly marked on Ordnance Survey maps. Access to the graveside is restricted because of its sensitive location in the heart of a private estate and can only be viewed by arrangement.

In the fourteenth century, Black Death, as the plague commonly became known, is estimated to have claimed forty-three million lives in Europe – perhaps one quarter of the world population. Whole crews died in the North Sea while in transit and the vessels with their sad cargoes drifted aimlessly on the deep. Many bodies were thrown into the rivers of Scotland. On the Continent, this also became such a popular mode of disposing of plague victims that the Pope was compelled to bless the River Rhône in order that the casting of corpses into its waters could be considered a form of Christian burial.

The widespread fear of being buried alive may have originated during times of plague when bodies were buried hurriedly – although this was probably a revival of a fear that has its roots in primeval human nature. Many plague victims, their families all already dead, kept linen cloth ready, into which they sewed themselves in their last moments. There are also almost incredible stories of plague victims lying in their graves and literally burying themselves to avoid being left unburied because they were the last survivors in the community.

Glasgow raised its defences several times in the late 1500s to meet a threat from the deadliest enemy ever to camp at its gates – plague. Too often these days 'plague' is carelessly used to describe modern scourges such as drug-related deaths and sexually-transmitted diseases. However, a glance through the early annals of Glasgow quickly shows how recurrent outbreaks of 'pest' touched everyone in a fearsome way which, we can only pray, will never be repeated.

Because of its cooler climate, Scotland actually escaped the worst ravages of the rodent-borne disease but plans made by Glasgow's city fathers to deal with an outbreak in the 1570s give some idea of the alarm which news of the arrival of plague occasioned.

When reports arrived that 'pest' was rife in Leith and the Fife ports, all traffic with these areas ceased immediately. Nobody from Glasgow was permitted to visit them and vice versa. And any citizen who went to Edinburgh was only allowed to return if they could supply a certificate of good health issued by the magistrates. All goods from the infected areas into Glasgow were to be forfeited and no stranger was to be admitted to the town without the permission of the magistrates. The bridge, the river and the four city gates were to be watched to ensure that neither infected persons nor goods should be smuggled into the town. Vagrant pipers, minstrels, fiddlers and strolling beggars were ordered to leave the town – non-compliance would result in a penalty of being branded on the cheek. A strict inquest was to be held into every illness and the master of the house was to report every case of sickness under pain of banishment.

However, while all these worthy measures were being taken, the population of rats that thrived on the dunghills, the piles of offal and the garbage-filled streets of Glasgow continued to grow.

Best calculations suggest that bubonic and pneumonic plagues, which affected Scotland from the mid fourteenth century until the end of the seventeenth century, carried off over 200,000 Scots (a sixth of the population) in its first wave and the final total may have run to as many as a million.

POISON

Over the centuries, we Scots have fine-tuned all sorts of horrendous methods of disposing of compatriots who failed to toe the politically correct line or simply omitted to buy their round. Every punishment imaginable from starvation (Duke of Rothesay, 1402) to multiple ventilation (David Rizzio, 1566) and lots of sinister stuff between times – burning, explosives, disembowelling, hanging, beheading and the infamous use of cairthorses to drag folk tae bits – has, at one time or another, been meted out.

But, for Scots, nothing held such terror as poisoning, known as 'the Italian trick', a means of 'sending men to the other world in figs and possets'. Figs and possets was an alcoholic cold remedy. Its strong taste meant it was perfect for disguising the fact that it had been adulterated with poison. Murder by poison was the ultimate terror – it could lead to a sudden, inexplicable choking death or, maybe worse, a creeping, insidious end.

In the year 1676, in one of the most sensational cases of the decade, it was two Edinburgh boys, Clark and Ramsay, aged seventeen and fifteen, who reminded us of this peculiarly Scottish fear. Ramsay worked for John Anderson, a city merchant. According to the chronicler Sir John Lauder of Fountainhall, Anderson had been labouring under an 'enfeebling malady' which in time was likely to have brought him to his grave. During his sickness, the two boys started to steal jewellery and other valuable items from the invalid, trusting he would, eventually, inevitably die and their crimes would never come to light. However, Anderson, contrary to all expectation and medical opinion, began to pick up. The boys became terrified and took another lad called Kennedy into the plot. He was an apothecary's assistant and supplied a drug which, when fed to Anderson in small doses, effected a successful relapse and he eventually died.

Initially, there was no suspicion of foul play until one of the boys greedily and stupidly tried to sell a gold chain that had formed part of their plunder. Sir John Clerk of Penicuik, a nephew of the murdered merchant, claimed that, while the crime was still undiscovered, he heard a voice urging him to 'avenge the blood of [his] uncle'. Shortly afterwards, he came across Anderson's chain in a goldsmith's shop and it was easily traced back to the two boys. Being detained and questioned, they apparently fell into such a terror that they readily confessed everything.

The boys were hanged and for months afterwards there was much anxious talk in the taverns of the capital and around the Mercat Cross that this 'Italian trick' might have come across the seas and would be widely used in Scotland.

POLITICS

Murder as a political expedient is a common enough phenomenon in Scotland. But, in 1714, a rather unusual spin on this is encountered. Campbell of Lochnell had died around 10 January but his son, a Jacobite, decided to keep the old man above ground until the end of the month. The reasoning behind this was to allow the gathering for the funeral to swell and, by doing this, the support for the Stuarts in exile would be so much greater. Interestingly, government supporters deemed it equally important to attend in order to show support for the establishment. As the *Analecta Scotica* records:

> Hence it came to pass, that the inhumation of Lochnell was
> attended by two thousand five hundred men, well-armed and
> appointed, five hundred being of Lochnell's own lands,

191

commanded by the famous Rob Roy, carrying with them a pair of colours belonging to the Earl of Breadalbane, and accompanied by the screams of thirteen bagpipes.

Such a subject for a picture!

POLLUTION

In 1608, the Convention of Royal Burghs, having examined the problem of pollution in the Clyde and its adverse effects on the salmon and trout fishing in the river, met in Selkirk. Following the meeting, Glasgow, Dumbarton and Renfrew were asked to severely punish individuals who were dumping 'deid careonnes' (carrion), 'buckeis' (bodies) and 'ither sic filth' in the river. Bearing in mind the importance of the salmon fishing to the nation at the time, this was clearly seen as a grave offence. However, we should never forget that the worst pollution of the river occurred during the industrial revolution two centuries and more later.

POPULARITY

In the 1830s, the Scot Patrick Logan was the unpopular and brutal commandant of Australia's Moreton Bay Penal Colony (Brisbane). When he was speared to death by Aborigines and eaten by wild dogs, it was said that convicts 'manifested insane joy, sang and hoorayed all night in defiance of the warders'. Since that day, Logan's ghost has occasionally been seen, sitting immobile, always on the far shore of the Brisbane River.

POST-MORTEM SNOBBERY

At Abernethy in 1647, the laird of Innerethy got a hard time for having buried his wife within the confines of the church, a long-established practice but one which the Reformed Church frowned on. He was given a serious talking-to despite the fact that his 'ancestors had been in possession of a place of burial there for the space of four hundred years'.

The absence of gravestones from the 1600s or earlier in Scottish burial grounds is a puzzle for most casual visitors to local kirkyards. The fact is that, in the seventeenth century, the interior of the church was still the place to be buried if you thought yourself somebody. However, the wise old greybeards of the kirk had realised that this could be a wee earner and decided to make the ambitious, wealthy members of the congregation pay for the privilege. Ordinary parishioners had to make do with 'God's Acre' surrounding the church.

In the records of the kirk at Invera'an in Strathspey was found an entry from August 1635 ordaining that no 'corps sall be letten in the kirk till 5lbs be payd before they get entres'.

The practice of burial under the floors of churches was prohibited by the General Assembly of the Church of Scotland in October 1582 but there does seem to have been difficulty controlling this age-old practice. Certainly, in the early days of the Reformation, the issue of burying inside the church was regarded with extreme displeasure and seriousness by the stern leaders of the kirk – they saw it, quite simply, as profanity. In February 1592, James Alexander from the parish of Logie, west of Stirling, appeared before the Presbytery and admitted that he had arranged for his wife Margaret to be buried inside the kirk but in turn blamed the elders and deacons for giving the go-ahead. This brought all sorts of problems for the ten elders

193

and deacons of Logie who found themselves severely censured. The threat of that most horrible of sentences, excommunication, was held over them until the whole squad and James Alexander publicly repented.

POSTPONING THE INEVITABLE

Scots have always claimed to have special knowledge when it comes to living a long life and keeping the Grim Reaper at bay. For instance, you'll hear folk tell you how ten cups of tea a day keeps you in the land of the living – while others will tell you that long life is guaranteed by abandoning tea altogether. The formulae are endless. One Scots-born frontiersman, who had lived through the hard days of the Old West, advised his grandson that if he wanted to live a long life then he should sprinkle gunpowder on his porridge every morning. The grandson did this faithfully for three score years and died leaving eight children, twenty-eight grandchildren, thirty-nine great-grandchildren – and a fifteen-foot hole in the wall of the crematorium.

POULTRY

William Anderson (b. 1746), a Provost of Stirling, often spoke of how he wished above everything else to die in office so that his coffin could be carried in splendour to the kirkyard, followed by the town council, council officers, guildry and trades. He got his wish. However, the cortege was not as dignified as the old man had hoped. Carried shoulder high through the town, the coffin had Willie's cocked hat displayed on the lid. In Baker Street, a hen which had been closed in by the crowds of onlookers could find no escape route so took to her wings, landing full square on the provost's headgear where she immediately set up a furious keckling. The smiles from the mourners and crowd in general broke the fierce solemnity of the occasion.

POVERTY

O Death! The poor man's dearest friend,
The kindest and the best!

Robert Burns (1759–96)

In the pre-Reformation period, the poor had no masses said for them when they died – hence the saying, 'Poor men hae nae souls.'

PRACTICALITY

We know that Mary, Queen of Scots rather too causally went off for a game of golf within a few hours of the murder of her husband, Henry Darnley. However, this practical, if slightly tough, streak seems to be built into the Scottish psyche. The story is told of the two golfers putting out on the eighteenth green at their local club. One of the men lifted his head from a crucial stroke, removed his golf cap and watched as a funeral procession passed by. His pal says, 'Alec, that was a decent thing to do. And you just needing to sink that to win.'

The golfer, returning to his putt, responded, 'It was the least I could do – I was married to her for forty years.'

Apocryphal that one perhaps but there is a traditional story in Westray, Orkney that would seem to bear out the idea. An old farmer was busy making a coffin for his wife who had died that same day when a cry of 'Whales in the bay' went up. When the laird arrived at the shore to oversee the catch, he was surprised to find the bereaved farmer in among the action and told him so. The farmer's response was, 'I couldna afford to lose both wife and whales on the same day.'

PRAGMATISM

The very practical, realistic streak in the Scot is obvious in the observation that 'Young folk may dee, but auld folk maun dee'.

PREMATURE BURIALS

The practice of watching the dead developed in Scotland into the phenomenon of lykewakes (waiting for the supposed dead to wake) and arose from an ancient, even primeval, fear of being buried alive. It is said that, in the early Middle Ages, during episodes of plague when burial space was at a premium, graves were dug up and the old bones were conveyed to an ossuary to free up burial space. Estimates suggested that one in every twenty-five coffins uncovered in this manner, chillingly, showed evidence of scratch marks . . . on the inside. Before the advent of devices such as the ECG, people in comas or trances were often mistakenly taken to be dead and premature burial was a frequent occurrence.

Over the centuries, all sorts of bizarre precautions were taken to avoid the ultimate nightmare of premature burial. These included:

† Signalling devices such as bells on the surface connected to a cord in the coffin in order that the recently buried could signal that a mistake had been made. It is thought that the phrases 'saved by the bell' and 'dead ringer' originated from this practice.
† Mutilation of bodies was conducted to ensure that any last vestige of life had been snuffed out.
† Holding mortuaries allowed a 'lying' time to ensure death had taken place.
† As well as having a hygienic function, washing the body was designed to help confirm the death.
† Calling to the dead – shouting the deceased's name loudly in their lughole – was designed to shock someone thought to be in a coma back to the land of the living. That it might equally give a comatose person heart failure does not seem to have been considered.
† A simple and obvious, if drastic, method practised was to leave the body around until it started to rot. Hence the auld saying, 'Uncle Tam's high theday'!
† Pouring hot metal on the deceased's most sensitive areas was occasionally employed to confirm death. Ouch!!
† Boiling liquids were similarly used. They were poured liberally into various orifices in an attempt to provoke a reaction. Ouch again!!
† Another technique, similar to, but more structured than, mutilation, was dissection. Removal of one or more of the vitals or complete dismemberment and removal of the heart or brain, more or less guaranteed an accurate diagnosis of death.

† A technique similar to 'calling to the dead' was to play 'Donald Whaur's Yer Troosers?' full blast over and over again to the deceased. This method appears to have had remarkable success in wakening not only the comatose but the truly deceased.

Open the Lid – I'm Feeling Better

In 1717, people learned with amazement of minister John Gardner who lived and died in Elgin. He was about to be buried when he woke in his coffin, knocked for the lid to be lifted and stunned grieving family and friends by climbing out of his box.

What Are You Waiting For?

Greeks, Hebrews and early Christians all thought that three days was the appropriate period to leave a body unburied, simply to ensure that the death had actually transpired. The Romans, on the other hand, were taking no chances – they would wait for up to eight days.

Not Dying but Sleeping

Here's some useful information for those still fearful of being planted prematurely. Complaints that can produce a death-like trance include:

Asphyxiation
Watching *River City*
Smallpox
Influenza
Negotiating the M8 at Townhead in the rush hour
Cholera

Epilepsy
Supporting Aberdeen FC during Steve Paterson's reign as manager
Shock
Apoplexy
Cerebral Anaemia
Listening to First Minister Jack McConnell
Catalepsy
Freezing
Being struck by lightning

DYING TO GET OUT

John Duns Scotus, or John of Duns, the Scottish cleric, who died c. 1308, looks to have been a victim of premature burial. This Borderer, who was one of Europe's greatest medieval philosophers, was held in contempt by some rivals. His defence of the theory of Immaculate Conception and his advocacy of blind faith led to his followers being ridiculed and called enemies of learning – hence the word 'dunce' was coined. He died in Cologne, where he had won great renown as the 'subtle doctor', but was found, some weeks after his supposed death, outside his coffin. It was noted that his hands were badly torn by efforts to prise the door of the vault open.

GRANDPA DOES NOT GO QUIETLY

Stories of people rising from apparent death are surprisingly common in the old texts. There is a tale from the far north of an old Highlander who appeared to have passed on. His son headed off to arrange the funeral and dig the grave. While he was away, his seven-year-old daughter, dumb from birth, came running through, saying,

'Mother, Mother, Grandfather is getting up!'

Terrified by this double miracle – the dumb child speaking and the dead man rising – the mother ushered the whole family to an outhouse and locked the door. Sure enough grandfather climbed down from his bier shouting, 'I'm coming – I've got you.' He started to scrape a hole under the door, scrabbling away like a dog. A trusty cockerel is said to have crowed and the old man fell back, stone dead – this time for good.

No Clowning Around

So afraid of being buried prematurely was Joseph Grimaldi, the famous English clown, that he left explicit instructions for his decapitation before burial.

Knock, Knock

Scotland has many strange tales of premature burial. On my home island of Papa Westray in Orkney, there is a spine-chilling legend of the Traills of Holland. The Traills were the often despotic lairds of the island. For three hundred years, they ruled the roost to such an extent that folk had to ask permission at the big hoose before they could leave the island.

One young man, kicking against the traces, upped and left without a word to the laird. Years later, he returned and, when Traill heard of this, he went to the pier to confront this precocious person who had had the nerve to take himself off to sea without so much as a by your leave. It was no slip of a boy that he met but a strong, fit young man. The story goes that Traill lifted his riding crop to strike the man but was floored by a haymaker of a punch. He was carried back to the house on the hill and not a trace of life could be found.

Arrangements were made for the funeral and, on the day appointed, Traill's box was carried down the dirt track to the kirkyard of St Boniface. As the coffin was humphed to the west shore, a knocking was heard from the interior. Intent on their task, the island lads carried on to the grave and the despot was duly put to his 'rest'. It seems likely that a form of cataleptic trance was responsible for this strange episode. And, with instances of collapse and apparent death being common during plague, cholera and smallpox outbreaks, mistakes were perhaps inevitable.

Thankfully, though, there are amusing anecdotes on topics of waking from apparent death. One story, which I'm assured is Scottish but which has been filched by various cultures, tells of the coffin of the wife of a hen-pecked husband being cairted to the kirkyard when it accidentally struck a dyke on a sharp corner. To the astonishment of the funeral party, the jolt roused the 'deceased' from her trance. According to tradition, she went on to live for several years but, when she died (for real this time) and the cortege passed the same spot, the husband whispered anxiously to the coffin bearers, 'Tak' tent o' the corner this time.'

This sort of story was deep-seated enough to be carried with the Scottish emigrants to North America among other places. Colin Lindsay was born in 1744 and was minister in the Sandhills area of North Carolina. He told how, back in Scotland, eight years before he was born, his mother had gone into a deep coma. Thought to be dead, she was buried near her Highland home. Thieves, anxious to steal her rings, dug up her body that same night and, when they couldn't prise a ring loose, tried to cut off her finger. You can imagine the dismay of the grave robbers when, at this painful moment, she regained consciousness . . . and sat up. The villains soon got off their marks. This story is now part of the folklore of the Carolinas.

PREMONITIONS

Strange deathbed premonitions are encountered in different periods of Scottish history. It is as if people who are close to death have shrugged off the restrictions of linear time and are able to peer into the future. In February 1566, just hours before Lord Henry Darnley, husband of Mary, Queen of Scots, was murdered at Kirk o' Field in Edinburgh, a Fife laird, John Lundin, lay gravely ill with a fever. He raised himself a little in his bed and cried out to those who attended him, 'Go help the king for the parricides are murdering him.' Later, Lundin declared, 'Now it is too late to help him, he is already murdered.' Lundin died soon afterwards.

Of course, the cynic might say that, so unpopular was Henry, such a prediction was scarcely stunning.

PRESENTATIONS

One feature of the American way of death that has not yet gained respectability in this country is the idea of the 'presentation'. Friends can visit and view the body either in the home or at the funeral parlour on the eve of the funeral. It is often a wee social evening with the deceased at the heart of the action. Apparently, this is necessary because it is much more difficult in the United States, certainly in the cities, to get time off work for the funeral of someone who is not a relative.

This can sometimes also be a problem in Scotland. The cold-heartedness of Scottish employers in relation to excessive absences was lampooned in a spoof letter that came my way recently. It was suggested that death (other than your own) is no excuse for absence

202

from work and pointed out that the company, in conjunction with the local authority, had launched a scheme for lunchtime burials, ensuring that no work time is lost. However, death (your own) is accepted as excuse for absence from work but the company would like two weeks' notice in order to train someone up for your job.

PULSE

When American painter Charles Peale was dying in 1827, he is reported to have asked his daughter to take his pulse. After a quick check she reported to her father that she could not find any. 'I thought not,' responded Charlie. These were his last words.

PUSHING YER LUCK

Wee Eck, who recently started as a warehoose gopher, is called in to see the boss. 'Eck, do you believe in life after death?' asks Mr Clootie.

'Aye sir,' the new recruit responds.

'That's fine then. Aifter you left early yesterday to go tae yer grandfaither's funeral, he stopped by tae see ye.'

In reality attending funerals, usually involving the loss of a grandparent, is one of Scotland's favourite excuses for missing work. Sickness is, as you would expect, the most common but research carried out nationally showed that one in five employees had, at one time or another, used the death of a loved one as an excuse for taking a time off. Remarkably, the vast majority of bosses accept such a plea for time off without question.

QUARRELS

A bitter argument between a husband and wife ended with Alec declaring, 'When you die, I'm getting you a headstone that reads, "Here Lies My Wife – Cold as Ever".'

'Aye, OK', says Mary, 'when you die, I'll get you a stone that says, "Here Lies My Husband – Stiff at Last".'

QUESTIONS ON DEATH THAT NEED ANSWERING

Why is it necessary to nail down the lid of a coffin?
Why do they call it life insurance when it's all tied up with when you die?

QUOTES ON DEATH

Here is a batch of quotes relating to death which are either truly Scottish or carry an inherent sense of Scottishness in their attitudes on death, including some that I may have dreamed up and a batch from that honorary Scot, that daft genius, Woody Allen:

Flodden! Aye, that's got a nice ring tae it. Let's fight the bloody
English there.

James IV, King of Scots

Either this man is dead or my watch has stopped.

Groucho Marx

Is Death the last sleep? No – it is the last and final wakening.

Sir Walter Scott

Every man dies. Not every man really lives.

William Wallace *in Braveheart*

It's not that I'm afraid to die, I just don't want to be around when
it happens.

Woody Allen

Listen, Hare, me back's killing me. Why don't we just top a few
while they're still above surface instead o' digging them up?

William Burke, lazy grave-robber-turned-murderer

I don't want to achieve immortality through my work – I want to
achieve it through not dying.

Woody Allen

The Glorious Twelfth – aye, right! What's so glorious about
getting your arse blasted by a gang o' tweed suits wi' their mooth
fu' o' marbles?

A Highland grouse, 11 August

I don't believe in an afterlife, although I am bringing a change of underwear.

Woody Allen

Alec: 'Life's too short to worry aboot death.'
Tam: 'Aye, that's whit worries me.'

Quotes on Death — International

It's passed on. This parrot is no more. It has ceased to be. It's expired and gone to see its maker. This is a late parrot. It's a stiff. Bereft of life. It rests in peace. If you hadn't nailed it to the perch it would be pushing up daisies. It's rung down the curtain and joined the choir invisible. THIS is an ex-parrot.

John Cleese *Monty Python's Flying Circus*

For life in the present there is no death. Death is not an event in life. It is not a fact in the world.

Ludwig Wittgenstein (1889–1951)

Death is nature's way of telling you to slow down.

Graffito

Ancient Egyptians believed that upon death they would be asked two questions and their answers would determine whether they could continue their journey in the afterlife. The first question was: 'Did you bring joy?' The second was: 'Did you find joy?'

Leo Buscaglia

My third question might be: 'Who's got the right answers?'

Death Valley is neither dead nor a valley.

Jerry Bunin

Life is pleasant. Death is peaceful. It's the transition that's troublesome.

Isaac Asimov

What we have done for ourselves alone dies with us; what we have done for others and the world remains immortal.

Albert Pike

Om Asatoma Sadgayama,
Tamasoma Jyoti Gamaya,
Myrityoma Amritam Gamaya.

From delusion lead me to truth,
From darkness lead me to light,
From death lead me to eternal light.

Hindu prayer

It's a funny old world – a man's lucky if he can get out alive.

W C Fields

Death is not extinguishing the light; it is putting out the lamp because dawn has come.

Rabindranath Tagore

Dying seems less sad than having lived too little.

Gloria Steinem

On the plus side death is one of the few things that can be done as easily lying down.

Woody Allen

Our fear of death is like our fear that summer will be short, but when we have had our swing of pleasure, our fill of fruit, and our swelter of heat, we say we have had our day.

Ralph Waldo Emerson

As the poets have mournfully sung,
Death takes the innocent young,
The rolling-in money,
The screamingly funny,
And those who are very well hung.

W H Auden

For what is it to die? But to stand in the sun and melt into the wind? And when the earth has claimed our limbs, then we shall truly dance.

Kahlil Gibran

The purpose of a funeral service is to comfort the living. It is important at a funeral to display excessive grief. This will show others how kind-hearted and loving you are and their improved opinion of you will be very comforting. As anyone familiar with modern fiction and motion pictures knows, excessive grief cannot be expressed by means of tears or a mournful face. It is necessary to break things, hit people, and throw yourself on top of the coffin, at least.

P J O'Rourke

Death is the most beautiful adventure in life.

Charles Frohman

If you should die before me, ask if you could bring a friend.

Stone Temple Pilots

I have never killed a man but I have read many obituaries with great pleasure.

Clarence Darrow

For three days after death, hair and fingernails continue to grow but phone calls taper off.

Johnny Carson

I didn't attend the funeral but I sent a nice letter saying I approved of it.

Mark Twain

Learn as if you were going to live forever and live as if you were going to die tomorrow.

Anon.

Eternity is a terrible thought. I mean, where's it going to end?

Tom Stoppard

If you were going to die soon and had only one phone call to make, who would you call and what would you say? And why are you waiting?

Stephen Levine

When I look back on all these worries, I remember the story of the old man who said on his deathbed that he had had a lot of trouble in his life, most of which had never happened.

Sir Winston Churchill

Dying is the most embarrassing thing that can ever happen to you, because someone's got to take care of all your details. You'd like to help . . . but you're dead, so you can't.

Andy Warhol

I don't believe people die from hard work. They die from stress and worry and fear – the negative emotions. Those are the killers, not hard work. The fact is, in our society today, most people don't understand what hard work is all about.

A L Williams

Be of good cheer about death and know this as a truth – that no evil can happen to a good man, either in life or after death.

Socrates

Raising the Dead

One of the last exponents of the black art of taghairm, consulting the dead for word of the future, was Alasdair MacTain, 'Ic Tain', who flourished at Ballimtombuy in the Loch Ness area at the beginning of the eighteenth century. His technique was to climb into a large cauldron, at the entrance to the burying ground of Clachan Mheircheird, and, from there, he summoned the dead to rise and pass before him until one appeared who could communicate the information he sought. On one occasion, when he was making a particularly bold attempt to solve the mysteries of the future, the dead rose and streamed into the surrounding fields in their thousands. The seer, however, could persuade no one to pass on the information he was looking for. At last, the form of his own dead niece appeared and spelled out the evils that would befall her uncle.

He is said to have never practised this dark art again but, in time, the girl's prophecies duly came to pass. Alasdair was gunned down by a group of Lochaber men who were stealing his cattle. He fell three times before he finally expired and the places where he fell are each marked by a cairn. Exactly what possible value he gained in learning his destiny is still a question worth asking.

A top witch once hung out in a lonely, forlorn spot near the Butt of Lewis. However, she was seldom lonely with her army of cats and two remarkable witchery skills. She was a dab hand at selling fair winds to sailors (released by unravelling a knot on a rope apparently) and she had a subtle skill that never goes wrong at a party – the ability to raise the dead. So you get the picture – when there wasn't a bunch of sailors waiting around at the back door, there was a procession of the spirits, conjured up by our witch, dressed and speaking exactly as they did when alive.

For one ambitious client, a huntsman, she agreed to call the spirit of the legendary Highland huntsman Fionn and his dog Bran. But it seems she was incapable of calling the dead back on her own behalf. So she hoped that Fionn would bring her insights into the world beyond the veil – the greatest secrets of the universe. Instead, when summoned, brave Fionn immediately launched into a conversation with his fellow huntsman about the best way of approaching a herd of red deer and the appropriate medicines to be given to the pack of hunting dogs. The old witch, it is said, was fair put out by this turn of events. Her demeanour wasn't helped by the fact that the great hunting dog Bran, scourge of the dark forests, ignored her cats and quietly settled down for a sleep at his master's feet.

REALITY BITES

The Civil War in America and the advent of photography saw Alex Gardner from Paisley come to prominence. He was a pioneer of the art and a critic in the *New York Times* wrote in 1862 that, in effect, Gardner had brought the bodies of those who fell on the battlefields of Antietem and Gettysburg and 'laid them on our doorstep'.

The view of many experts in the field is that a last look at the deceased is therapeutic for adults and children alike – that moments of truth when the living confront the dead help people grieve by facing the harsh reality that there is no return.

REFUGE

For some time now, despite the fall in church attendance, undertakers in Scotland invariably find that, when they ask what religion the deceased was, they are told 'Church of Scotland'. This is simply because so many people, who have not darkened the door of the kirk for decades, are alarmed at the response of friends and neighbours if they were to organise a funeral where God did not get an invite.

REGISTRATION

In Scotland, the law requires that a death is registered within eight days. In England, Wales and Northern Ireland the period is five days. Could this be a legacy of the difficulties in reaching a registrar in far-flung Highland glens during the depths of winter? Another difference in death registration north of the Border is that here the death must be registered not only in the district where it occurred but also in the area of Scotland where the deceased normally lived. In the majority of cases this is one and the same thing.

RELATIVE COMFORT

On a frozen winter Sunday two Highlanders emerge from the kirk in

Strathspey to be met by an icy blast from the north. Angus coughs loud and long. Says Donald to Angus, 'Man, that's a bad cold you have there, Donald.'

'Aye,' sniffs his companion, looking round wistfully at the snow falling on the crowded graveyard, 'but there's a few in here who would be glad o' it.'

RELIGION

Muslims do not use Scottish undertakers as funeral directors because, under the laws of the Koran, their holy book, the undertakers are unclean and cannot be allowed to handle the Muslim dead.

REPLICATION

In the 700s St Fillan died on the shores of Loch Earn and a crowd from Glen Dochart went to bring his body back. They had negotiated Glen Ogle and the party was resting at a spot where tracks to Strath Fillan and Killin diverge when it occurred to someone present that it would be as well to decide exactly where the holy man should be buried. A scrap seemed on the cards when suddenly it was noticed that two coffins had appeared, one on each side of the road. This miraculous solution to the difficulty allowed both groups of the saint's admirers to conduct peaceful ceremonies at two sites.

St Baldred in East Lothian appears to have gone a step further. When three villages contested the right to retain his remains, he succeeded in producing two duplicates.

REQUESTING DEATH

In the 1600s, when witch burning was more common than it should have been, it occasionally seems to have been an avenue for legal suicide. Let me explain. An old man in Edinburgh gave himself up and produced a detailed confession of his warlock activity. He pleaded, earnestly, to be executed for the 'safety of his saul'. He got his wish and was burned at the stake.

Even sadder are the reports of the trial of Bessie Graham of Kilwinning who denied all the charges laid against her but sadly, and innocently, admitted to her persecutors that there were so many accusations against her that she fully understood why they thought her guilty. Although there is no record of her fate, she was, in all likelihood, burned.

RESPONSES TO DEATH

Well into the twentieth century, the rituals of death varied not just from region to region within Scotland but almost from village to village. However, one of the shared characteristics was that death invariably took place at home and there were some universally accepted procedures which had to be followed in the minutes immediately after a bereavement – the dos and don'ts of death, if you like. These responses may seem bizarre when set against our contemporary 'hands-off' way of coping with a family death but they were all designed to speed the spirit of the deceased on its way. Broadly the rules were:

† Do open all the windows and doors in order to set the newly released spirit free

† Do stop the clocks and only restart them after interment
† Do cover furniture with sheets and drapes – preferably black ones
† Don't leave any mirrors in the house uncovered, in order that the newly freed spirit doesn't see itself, get confused and refuse to vacate the premises
† Don't remove the body from house head first or the spirit might see the way back into the house

The modern Scottish way of handling a death in the family setting bears no resemblance to these superstitious, hands-on old ways. The common response now is roughly like this:

† Burst oot the greetin' by all means – but quietly, please
† Shut all the doors and windows and draw the curtains
† Call the undertaker immediately
† Don't touch or, above all, look at the body
† Under no circumstances keep the coffined body in the house
† Forget all about the deceased's wish for a burial
† Keep the children well away from the corpse
† Call the minister whom you haven't seen for years

Sadly, but fortunately for most of us who run scared from death (and that is most of us), family and friends now generally and conveniently die away from our precious clean and ordered domesticity, in care – either in a hospital or a nursing home – and the professionals immediately take over. It is also a fact that weddings and funerals are often the only times extended families meet. The experience of the experts in the field is that funerals too often tend to bring out the worst out in folk.

Resting Places

Although stone cairns were the most familiar kind of resting place for the funeral cortege to park their coffin, wells also served as halts. At Madderty in Southwest Perthshire, on an old road to the parish burying ground, stands 'The Croonin' Well' which is believed to have been used first by a community of monks based nearby. It may have been that, in later years, it was a handy place to divvy oot the oatcakes and get some water for your whisky during the long trek to the kirkyard.

Restless Dead

On an island in the Clyde the local cemetery needed to expand. As a short-term measure, part of an adjacent field was commandeered from a local farmer. Here bodies were to be temporarily laid to rest until the new yard opened. Despite the advice of the farmer that the site wasn't suitable, the council pressed ahead, hinting that they considered the location ideal and he should stick to what he knew about – farming. Two funerals took place and again the farmer tried to stress the unsuitability of the site but to no avail.

When the new yard became available arrangements were made for the disinterment of the two burials so that they could make the last leg of their journey to their final resting place. Gravediggers arrived on site but, after hours of excavation, they could not trace the remains. The farmer watched the activity from the sidelines. Once they had dug down eight feet and officials were already trying to frame excuses for family and the media, the farmer again stepped forward. His advice this time was to check the adjacent field. It took some significant persuasion but, when they dug nearby, they soon discovered the burials. As it turns out, the site was originally a peat bog and it was known for buried items to migrate from place to place underground. Due to the nature of the soil the farmer had previously lost the remains of a couple of heifers in the same way.

Rest Stops

According to my straw poll of Scottish undertakers it is a rare event indeed now for a family to keep the body of the deceased in the house before the funeral. It is calculated that, before burial and cremation, something like 99 per cent of bodies 'rest' in the funeral parlours.

Resuscitation

The bumpy road to Musselburgh was responsible, say most experts, for bringing Maggie Dickson, who had had her neck stretched in 1728 at the Grassmarket in Edinburgh for child murder (probably by abandoning a newly-born child), back to the land of the living. As she lay in a cart rattling over the cobbles, she sat up and survived to live a long life. Half-hingit Maggie, as she became known, has the ultimate honour of having a pub in the Grassmarket named after her.

That this was not a unique case is illustrated by the story of Ann Green who, in 1650, was found to be still breathing after being hanged. An executioner stamped on her chest and stomach with the intent of finishing her off but only managed to fully revive her.

Rich Man, Poor Man, Beggar Man

In 1638, Greyfriars Churchyard in Edinburgh was scene of the first signing of the Covenant and it is, perhaps, Scotland's most famous kirkyard. The register of burials that had taken place there in the second half of the seventeenth century offers an insight into the lives and deaths of the citizens of Edinburgh and gives a feel for the character of the city at that time. Among the cryptic entries in the records are the following:

† Robert Orr, writer, a bastard, buried, August 20, 1674
† Lord Pressmannan, buried in the kirk, November 13, 1695
† Thomas Lilborir, withachrist (witchcraft?), executed December 14, 1666
† Cuthbert Ogilvie, Englishman from the College, buried January 13, 1669
† Andrew Russell, a merchant of Amsterdam, buried November 16, 1697
† William Wallace, interred in the bernsknow (the infants' burial mound), June 28, 1694.

Rocks

There is a widely held belief that change, even for more transient features of the landscape like the Old Man of Hoy, is a gradual one. Not so. Set against the human lifespan, rock, of course, may seem everlasting but this is an illusion. The sandstone pillar on the island of Hoy is being eroded at its base and a catastrophe is not impossible. The fragility of the landscape thereabouts indicates that rock, like human flesh, must also eventually give way to time.

Greyfriars Churchyard

This is also in evidence on my home island of Papa Westray, right on the northern fringe of the Orkney group. We once had a magnificent cavern, a cathedral-like place called the Ha's o' Habbrahellya. One morning, in the 1950s, an islander passed the cave on his way to the creels and, on his return, he was stunned to discover that it had collapsed into the sea.

It's said, in legend, that the Old Man of Hoy was a giant who was turned to stone because he lingered too long on the tideline while night fishing and was fossilised by the first rays of the morning sun. The truth is rather less dramatic. A hydrographical survey of the Hoy coast, as recent as 1770, made no mention of the stack or stacks so a headland must presumably have been in place then. And an engraving from the beginning of the nineteenth century shows the Old Man standing on two legs. But, by 1935, one writer was predicting the demise of the Old Man. So far, he has defied the prophets of collapse but, in time, this Old Man will go the way of all of us.

Maybe the single biggest sadness about a sudden doonfa' of the Old Man would be the fact that George Mackay Brown is no longer around to record the event – but maybe the collapse would encourage the blossoming of his successor. You never know.

RUNNING FUNERALS

Petty or Pettie is a parish on the Moray Firth north-east of Inverness. It was the bizarre habit in this parish to run as fast as possible with the coffin from the home of the deceased to the grave. As a result of this energetic sprint, peching and panting mourners were often left by the roadside. It gave rise to an old saying which urged an increased pace – 'Let's tak' a Pettie step to it.'

SABBATH BREAKING

A 'very scandalous' breach of the Sabbath was reported at Errol in Perthshire in October 1701. Apparently this involved carrying a corpse from the parish of Kinnoul to the churchyard of Errol during the time of public worship. In 1724, in the same parish, a wright was reported to the Presbytery for making a coffin for a child that had died during Saturday/Sunday night. Hard times, indeed.

SAFER BY RAIL

In the Victorian era, so confident were the burgeoning railway companies of being in the midst of a travel/tourist boom that they were prepared to accept adverts for Aberdeen granite headstones in their bright and breezy promotional literature.

SCARED TO DEATH

What is currently the most terrifying death-related phenomenon in Scotland? Hundreds of people, Scots and foreign visitors alike, will nominate the Mackenzie Mausoleum in Greyfriars Churchyard, Edinburgh, as the scariest place in twenty-first-century Scotland. And they have the scars to prove it.

Jan-Andrew Henderson, director of City of the Dead Tours, says quite openly that, before setting up the tour, they looked around for a supernatural phenomenon that was becoming notorious. That entity is the so-called Mackenzie Poltergeist. 'I wanted people to go along somewhere and know that the experience they were getting might actually be genuine,' he says. What followed was remarkable. First of all, a unique partnership was struck with Edinburgh Council to open up the Covenanters Prison in the graveyard. The graveyard is rented from the council in exchange for permission to conduct the tours and, in that sense, the graveyard is paying its way. Says Jan-Andrew, 'As someone in the council once pointed out to me, the council can't make money out of graveyards. This way, we pay them.'

Events in and around the tomb of Sir George Mackenzie of Rosehaugh (1639–91), much-hated prosecutor of the Covenanters, are even more remarkable. The Covenanters Prison has always had a famous reputation for being haunted – even Robert Louis Stevenson wrote about it. Dozens of faintings, a catalogue of minor injuries to visitors and strange sightings have been reported. Jan-Andrew explains, 'I've seen people collapsing several times in there and I've seen cuts and scratches on people's bodies immediately after their visit to the mausoleum. I didn't see these marks appear so I suppose they could have done that themselves – again, I suppose it could be psychosomatic. I'm always in two minds about it. But it's an odd place. I don't know if the phenomenon is supernatural but it is definitely beyond what can be explained at the moment.'

He is unabashed at the blatant commerciality of the operation. 'Greyfriars has a unique history and this is a rare opportunity for visitors to see around the prison, which is not normally open to the public, and to hear the stories of the place. I think people come on the "dead" tour because we genuinely have something that cannot be explained and, despite formal religion seeming to have lost its hold and science tearing apart old theories, folk still love the idea of life after death, something beyond the grave.'

SECOND SIGHT

This strange ability – *an da sheallach* in Gaelic – was considered to be inherited and was generally recognised to be connected with premonitions of death. Often this involved the sighting of an individual, known to be in another part of the country or even on another continent, at his own front door or the appearance of a bed-ridden individual at one of his or her old haunts. The reading of these visitations is that the person sighted is about to die or has died. Occasionally, according to Bruford, the seer (*taibhsear*) might find himself confronted by a phantom funeral cortege. Reports also speak of the ability of the seer to predict where the body of a dead individual might be carried ashore by the tide or whether a missing boat would return safely. Interestingly, it is thought many, perhaps all, of us have this undeveloped gift. Right into the twenty-first century, feyness, the characteristic of people fated to die soon, is still said to be observed by those with the gift.

SECURITY

In Mull, after a death in the family, a sprig of pearlswort was placed above the lintel of the front door in the belief that this prevented the spirit of the deceased from re-entering the house.

SHAKESPEARE AND DEATH

Naturally enough the Bard of Avon, who explored every aspect of life and human relationships in minute detail, had some important observations on life's greatest certainty. Here are my favourite Shakespearean sayings on the nature of death, dying and the dead:

How oft when men are at the point of death
Have they been merry!
Which their keepers call
A lightning before death.

Romeo and Juliet, V.3

So shalt thou feed on Death, that feeds on men
And Death once dead, there's no more dying then.

'Sonnet 146'

What's brave, what's noble,
Let's do it after the High Roman fashion,
And make death proud to take us.

Antony and Cleopatra, IV.13

Cowards die many times before their deaths;
The valiant never taste of death but once.

Julius Caesar, II.2

Shake off this downy sleep, death's counterfeit,
And look on Death itself!

Macbeth, II.3

I am a tainted wether of the flock,
Meetest for death: the weakest kind of fruit
Drops earliest to the ground.

The Merchant of Venice, IV.1

For in that sleep of death what dreams may come
When we have shuffled off this mortal coil,
Must give us pause.

Hamlet, III.1

And all our yesterdays have lighted fools
The way to dusty death. Out, out, brief candle.

Macbeth, V.5

SHIFT WORK

In Scotland, coffin bearers worked in rotation to carry the deceased for up to 100 miles for burial near his or her ancestors. Even the aristocracy were cairted for long miles to their interment. Noted eighteenth-century Jacobite and poet Robertson of Struan died in 1749 and as many as 2,000 people attended his funeral. He was carried nineteen miles from his estate in Rannoch to the traditional family burying ground, four miles west of Blair Atholl. Earlier in the same century, the death of Lachlan, chief of the Clan Mackintosh, sparked off a programme of funeral entertainments which lasted a month before the burial. Aye, but how did they prevent the chief guest, the deceased, well past his sell-by date by that time, from contaminating the proceedings? The answer, for folk of importance who were often socially obliged to hang around above surface longer than might be wise, was embalming or filling their veins with a temporary preservative. Mackintosh's funeral in 1704 was notable also because the family brought cooks and chefs from Edinburgh to cope with the army of guests and, as usual, 'drink was set aflowing in the greatest profusion'. On the day of the interment, the procession is said to have stretched from Dalcross Castle to the kirk of Pettie, a distance of four miles! Expenditure on this funeral was a financial embarrassment to the family of the clan chief for a century afterwards.

Equally impressive was the 1729 funeral of Sir Robert Munro of Foulis, 'a very ancient gentleman'. We are told in the columns of the *Edinburgh Evening Courant* that four counties turned out to show their respect to the clan chief:

> There were above six hundred horsemen tolerably mounted and apparelled. The corpse was carried on a bier betwixt two horses, fully harnessed in deepest mourning. A gentleman rode in deep mourning before the corpse, uncovered, attended by two grooms and four running-footmen, all in deep mourning. The friends followed immediately behind the corpse and the strangers in the rear.

The reporter, who obviously got a wee bit carried away by the solemnity of the occasion, also noted, 'The scutcheons were the most handsome I ever saw; the entertainment magnificent and full.'

SHROUDS

By the 1680s, between 10,000 and 12,000 Scots were involved in the linen trade. As a protectionist measure in 1686, the Scottish Parliament passed an Act 'for burying in Scots linen'. This Act provided that all corpses should be buried 'in plain linen or cloth of hards [cloth made from the coarse refuse of flax, etc.] spun within the Kingdom'. The use of foreign cloth, specifically Dutch, was banned. Parish ministers were held responsible for seeing compliance with the Act.

SIDELINE ENTERTAINMENT

When the remains of Helen Lindsay, widow of Captain Campbell of Glenlyon in Perthshire, were laid out for burial at Chesthill around the early 1700s, there was a great gathering that lasted several days. The young men who had assembled passed the time by tossing the caber and putting the shot.

SIGNIFICANT SIGNPOST

This Is the Way to Heaven

This is the motto of the old burgh of Canongate in Edinburgh.

SIMILES AND METAPHORS

Death has always been useful as a way of describing certain conditions:

† Dead drunk
† Like death warmed up
† Dead to the world
† Dead as a doornail
† Deadpan

SIMPLICITY

The Reformed Church in Scotland's *First Book of Discipline* (1560–61) stated that it was 'judged best' that there should be no singing, reading or sermons at burials but that the dead should be carried to burial 'with some honest company of the Kirk . . . and committed to the grave without further ado'.

SIZE

Probably the largest woman of eighteenth-century Scotland was the wife of Captain Budd of Ford in Midlothian. She was buried in Greyfriars Churchyard in Edinburgh in a coffin that was reputed to be two feet deep.

It is an historical fact that William the Conqueror was too big for his coffin and that, in an unseemly struggle to squeeze him into his box, according to Tibball, his back was broken and his stomach exploded. Less well known is the fact that the Tenth Duke of Hamilton, anxious to be buried in style, spent thousands of pounds in the 1850s on an Egyptian sarcophagus. The chookie had, however, failed to take into account that the Egyptians were generally small of stature and it is said that the Duke's legs had to be severed post-mortem before he could be slotted into the coffin.

An open-air Highland sermon

Skulls

Ground human skull, or water mixed with the same and drunk from the crown of a skull, was given to epileptics in different parts of Europe to prevent seizures. The Highlands of Scotland had an unusual spin on this technique in that the skull of a suicide was used by preference and those apparently thus cured were never again permitted to touch a dead body or view a funeral.

Slips (of the Tongue)

As a young newspaper reporter, one of my regular tasks was to cover meetings of the district councils in West Dunbartonshire. One meeting of Vale of Leven District Council sticks in the mind. A very serious discussion was taking place on the broken-down state of the road leading to the local cemetery. One councillor got quite passionate about this problem, saying, 'I don't think the officials responsible for this state of affairs realise that, at one time or another, all of us here have gone up that road to bury our relatives and our dead.' Aye, well . . .

Smooching

Kissing or even touching a corpse in most European traditions is said to ensure good fortune for the living and allows the dead to rest in peace. Interestingly, it is also claimed that, by touching a corpse, all fear of death is removed.

At a much simpler level, the touch of a corpse's hand would cure warts – the theory being that the warts would die as the body decayed.

SNACKS FOR THE FUNERAL GUESTS

If you are in a wee quandary about whether to serve sausage rolls or tuna and cress sandwiches at the Uncle Hamish's wake, then take a leaf out of the handbook of social etiquette of some tribes in Africa and South America – and eat the deceased! For these peoples this is the most respectful way of disposing of your loved ones.

SOLUTIONS

There is a remedy for everything – except death.

Anon.

SOME SPECIALIST SCOTTISH DEALERS IN DEATH

Sir George Mackenzie of Rosehaugh – the much-detested persecutor of the Covenanters
Kenneth MacAlpin – the first King of Scots and probably the liquidator of the Picts
The Wolf of Badenoch (Alexander Stewart) – excommunicated troublemaker whose favourite hobby was terrorising market towns and burning cathedrals
Francis Stewart, Fifth Earl of Bothwell – attacked and terrorised royal residences and is said to have consorted with witches in a failed attempt to cause the death of James VI

The burning of Elgin Cathedral

Robert Knox – the anatomist who, as keeper of Edinburgh Anatomy Museum, was responsible for procuring hundreds of corpses, including those supplied by the notorious Burke and Hare

Campbell of Glenlyon – although the Earl of Stair took much of the flak for the Massacre of Glencoe in 1692, it was Campbell who put the orders into action

Earl Patrick Stewart of Orkney – ruled Orkney with an iron fist and was universally detested throughout the isles but he did have a nice palace built in Kirkwall

SOUVENIRS

The cremated remains of the novelist D H Lawrence were mixed with concrete and made into a mantelpiece for his girlfriend.

SPACE SAVERS

In the 1970s, it was calculated that the United Kingdom saved an area of ground equivalent to that of 607 football pitches through people choosing cremation over burial.

Areas in the vicinity of Scottish crematoriums have, over the years, been set aside for the disposal of items, such as artificial limbs, hip joints, etc., which cannot be burned for environmental reasons. Recently, however, these items have begun to be sent for re-cycling – thereby freeing up even more space.

Scottish battles as a pay-per-view spectator event is an interesting concept in this television age. From the comfort of our armchairs, we watched the Twin Towers fall and saw smart missiles jumping the traffic lights in downtown Baghdad. These horrendous happenings make for compulsive viewing. We may convince ourselves that there is serious intent in watching terrorist mayhem and artillery bombardments; that we have a moral obligation to make ourselves aware of the death-dealing which is a daily occurrence in this increasingly confusing world of ours. But the bottom line is that these events are live theatre.

This fascination with conflict is as old as warfare itself. In centuries past, without rock concerts, sporting events and political rallies, Scots would turn out to watch the battles which shaped the nation. It was a dangerous, occasionally fatal, pastime. Camp followers, especially women and children, suffered dreadfully during the Civil Wars in Scotland in the mid seventeenth century – most infamously at Methven, Kilsyth and Philiphaugh – and several incidents are also recorded in the 1745 Jacobite uprising. For example, it's known that, during the Battle of Culloden, the over-enthusiastic redcoats collared a group of sightseers from Inverness and put them to the sword.

When John Witherspoon was the minister at Beith in Ayrshire, he went along to the Battle of Falkirk and, along with several others, he was huckled in a sweep made by the Jacobites around the edge of the battlefield. From there, he was taken to Doune Castle and thrown into the deepest, darkest dungeon. But he eventually escaped and later became an emigrant signatory to the American Declaration of Independence. Another clergyman, the Rev. Alexander Carlyle, recorded how he watched the Battle of Prestonpans a few months earlier from the steeple of his kirk at Inveresk.

Possibly the most notorious loss of battle spectators in Scottish history took place in the course of the Battle of Glen Fruin on 8 February 1603, when Alastair McGregor of Glenstrae routed a force under his old rival Alexander Colquhoun of Luss in the lonely glen between Loch Lomond and the Gare Loch. The battle, more of a skirmish really, was over in a matter of minutes with 140 killed on the Colquhoun side, caught in a McGregor pincer action. Only two McGregors lost their lives.

According to tradition, forty scholars from the Grammar School in Dumbarton were massacred in cold blood. The town of Dumbarton had offered support to the Colquhouns and the boys had journeyed to the Glen of Sorrow to watch their fathers and brothers fight. Dugald Ciar Mhor is the man who gets the blame, even from the McGregors, for single-handedly slaughtering the boys, who had been taken prisoner before the battle. When asked after the fighting about the schoolboys, Ciar Mhor drew his bloodstained dirk that he'd used to kill them and said, 'Ask that and God save me!' Strangely, although the clan itself seems to have accepted that such a horrendous event did taken place, the general indictment against the McGregors does not mention this crime.

One other fascinating piece of evidence suggests that the killing of the scholars does have a basis in historical fact. As late as 1757, pupils at Dumbarton Academy took part in an odd ceremony on the anniversary of the battle. The dux of the school, wrapped in a shroud, was carried to the churchyard where a mock burial took place and Gaelic odes, referring to the massacre, were recited.

The McGregors were to suffer terribly for their victory. Twenty-five of them were later executed and the heads of the chief and one of his henchmen were displayed on the Tolbooth at Dumbarton. The McGregor clan, the 'children of the mist', were declared outlaws, their lands forfeited, their children moved to the Lowlands and the men forbidden to carry any weapon save a blunt knife to eat their meat with.

SPEEDY DEPARTURES

In Scotland, it is generally accepted that, given a straightforward death, we bury or cremate our dead fairly quickly. We certainly can't match the Middle Eastern countries where, in the stifling heat, there is a quite understandable urgency to get the deceased below ground in the shortest time possible.

SPORT

The statutes of the Scottish church of the thirteenth century prohibited wrestling and games in churches and churchyards – which suggests that a lot of fun could have gone on there in previous years. Concern that the kirkyards should be places of sanctuary and cleanliness is indicated by a diocesan synod held at Musselburgh, as early as 1242, ordering churchyards to be properly enclosed and protected against wild animals.

SQUARE GO

James IV, a man known for his devotion to the outmoded tenets of chivalry, is said, shortly before his downfall at Flodden, to have challenged the aged Earl of Surrey to single combat to avoid massive loss of life. As well as the return of Berwick, James wanted the removal of a lucrative salmon trap which the English had located on the River Esk. On such seemingly trifling matters rested the lives of thousands of men. James's offer was rejected by that wily old coyote Surrey. Clutching his walking frame, Surrey declared that, as a commoner, he could not cross swords with a king.

STARS IN THE BRIGHT SKIES

In a twentieth-century survey of attitudes to death, a sixty-year-old Scots shopkeeper, an enthusiastic of member of the kirk, went a wee bit further than some Presbyterian clergymen might. When asked about the afterlife, he earnestly insisted that the stars in the bright sky that look down from above are people who have gone before us, shining their light on the earth. But the shopkeeper's notion was nothing new. He was drawing on profound ideas that predate Christianity by many centuries. Plato, the great philosopher of Athens, suggested:

> Once you shone among the living as the Morning Star;
> Among the dead you shine now, as the Evening Star.

STRANGE PRACTICES

In 1641, the kirk session in Colinsburgh in Fife, acting on the instructions of the Presbytery, ordained that all those 'who superstitiously carry the dead about the kirk' before burial would be censured.

Home from the kirk

Odd, ancient traditions, such as carrying the coffin three times round the church, were known to have persisted.

SUICIDE

People who took their own lives were, of course, denied interment alongside other members of their community in consecrated ground. By tradition, in Scotland, they were normally buried 'where three lairds' lands meet'. This refusal to allow 'suicides' sacred burial was firmly established in the seventeenth century when one Angus minister bucked the trend and insisted on burying a suicide in his kirkyard. In an attempt to appease the superstitious parishioners, he is said to have jumped three times across the grave. However, following the minister's death and during a renovation of the kirk, the 'rebel' preacher's coffin was dug up and propped up against a wall. It seems the congregation were less than happy about having him interred beside their loved ones. Years passed and, as the coffin weathered, it became possible to glimpse the skeleton within. A successor in the pulpit eventually ordered the coffin – complete with occupant – to be taken off to a lonely spot and burned.

Suicide can often seem to be a disease of recent times but it figures in the records over the centuries as a way out for troubled individuals. In 1574, a public suicide shocked Edinburgh when a convicted adulterer, Robert Drummond, stabbed himself four times in the chest while he was undergoing punishment at the Mercat Cross.

It is reckoned that, every day, worldwide, 1,000 people commit suicide. In Japan suicide is like an epidemic. Incredibly, in Japan, close to 1,000 people commit suicide every year by setting fire to their homes. Debts and domestic problems are thought to be the principal motives.

An early plea in justification of suicide when life becomes intolerable came from eighteenth-century Scots philosopher David Hume. His work *Of Suicide* concluded with a sentiment with which most of us surely concur:

> I am only convinced of a matter of fact, which you yourself acknowledge possible, that human life may be unhappy, and that my existence, if further prolonged, would become ineligible: but I thank providence, both for the good which I have already enjoyed, and for the power with which I am endowed of escaping the ill that threatens me.

The myth of the happy Highlander, content with his or her lot, was shattered in the early 1990s by a government report which showed that more people committed suicide in the Highlands than in any other part of Scotland. Experts said the high rate of alcoholism and the culture of binge drinking were central factors in this worrying situation.

SUPERSTITION

Death, as the greatest mystery in life, was always edged around by strange and occasionally inexplicable superstitious practices. In Orkney, the feet of the corpse always had to point towards the door during the laying out and no lamp was allowed to go out between sunrise and sunset. A cross might be painted inside the door to keep malicious spirits away from the corpse. The body sometimes lay for as long as eight days before burial.

241

SUPPORT

Chairs and stools were often used to support the coffin as it lay in the best room during the lykewake. Throughout Scotland, the tradition was that these stools should be thrown over after the coffin had been lifted from them to ensure that they would not have to be used again soon.

SURGERY

During the Renaissance period, the art of surgery was fraught with danger. Henry Sinclair, Bishop of Ross, and an opponent of the Reformation, set off in the summer of 1563 for Paris in order to get 'remede of ane confirmed stane'. This seems to suggest that, in mid-sixteenth-century Scotland, there was no one able to perform a lithotomy . . . or perhaps the Bishop simply didn't trust a Reformer with a scalpel. Anyway, the reverend father was operated on by Laurentius, a noted surgeon in the French capital, but he caught a fever and died during the following winter. That charitable old greybeard, John Knox commented, 'God strake him according to his deservings.'

Taking it with You — or Not

The claiths o' the deed need nae pouches.

or to give the modern equivalent:

There's nae pockets in a shroud.

Taste

An American company does a roaring trade in toe tags – those identification labels that are used on corpses by funeral undertakers and mortuary staff. The idea is that, if someone passes out because they've overdone the drink, they will wake up to find themselves toe-tagged – scary! And, as if this wasn't bizarre enough, the company also offer a 'disaster' kit with twenty-five unprinted toe tags for those 'big, disastrous occasions'.

TEETH

Each year, it is calculated that crematoriums in Scotland belch out about 130 kg of mercury in vapour form. This is created when bodies with amalgam fillings are cremated. Effects of mercury poisoning, it is claimed, can range from mood swings and listlessness among adults to stillbirths. Research has confirmed that families living in close proximity to crematoriums and waste incinerators are at greater risk. Amalgam fillings came into use after the Second World War and, as the generation most affected begins to die off, the problem is expected to increase dramatically in the next decade.

As time passes, we share more and more with our partners. In old age, many of the things that separated us in youth unite us. One Clydeside funeral director was called in to help after the death of a man, one half of an elderly couple who were both well into their nineties and who had shared a happy life together. All the arrangements went as planned but it was only after the frail widow had been collected in the limo that the funeral director sensed something was amiss. From the woman's frequent facial contortions, he felt there was something more than the pain of grief going on. It turned out the funeral director had been supplied with her false teeth rather than her late husband's. After a brief delay at the crematorium, for a discreet switch, the old lady was reunited with her own wallies.

TERMINOLOGY

In the modern Western world, where death is successfully kept at a distance from the non-professional and normally occurs in hospital, sociologists have come to describe such deaths as 'medicalised'.

244

TERRORISM, ETC.

Man's inhumanity to man,
Makes countless thousands mourn!

'Man Was Made to Mourn' (1786)
Robert Burns (1759–96)

TESTING FOR DEATH –
SOME OLD AND NEW FAVOURITES

1. Relaxation of the sphincter muscles
2. Dull eyes and dilated pupils
3. No swelling in tied-off finger ends
4. No moisture on a mirror held over the nostrils
5. Absence of reflexes
6. Insensitivity to electrical stimuli
7. No reaction to noxious stimuli
8. Absence of blinking
9. The deceased feels like a slab of meat
10. Putrefaction – really the only sure sign

(*See* **Pulse** for reasons why this last one is strangely absent as a proof of death.)

TIDINESS

In 1995, a Kenyan Member of Parliament suggested that hyenas be introduced to clean up hospitals with no mortuaries by eating the bodies of the unclaimed dead. Chris Kamuyu made the suggestion when another MP complained that his district hospital had no public cemetery.

TIGHT-FISTEDNESS

The legendary but entirely mythical Scottish trait of money-grabbing meanness naturally enough follows us to the grave and beyond. The following was picked up in a surfing session on the internet:

> A thrifty Scots widow, her fisherman husband having passed away, arranges for the local undertaker to make a coffin from fish boxes. On her visit to the draper next door, she is stunned at the cost of material for a shroud, telling the draper she could buy similar cloth down the road for half the price. 'Aye, indeed,' replies the draper, 'but the stuff is of such poor quality that it'll wear through at the knees within the week.'

Interestingly, Anne Gordon tells of the Forfarshire pedlar who sold a shroud to an old woman but, when he returned the following week, she complained that it was so tight she couldn't draw breath in it.

Then there was a group of American tourists who were strolling through an Edinburgh boneyard when they encountered a headstone with the message:

> Here lies a pious man, a wonderful father, and a great teacher.

One of the visitors was heard to observe, 'Trust the Scots to bury three men in one grave.'

TOMBSTONES

Scotland's thousands of graveyards, among them some of the most scenic in the world, have a wonderful array of decorated tombstones. Originally, headstones were designed to keep the dead from wandering. By the 1700s, the symbols of death were a very necessary part of the design of tombstones and were displayed with great effect. Skulls, cross-bones, winged cherubs, sand glasses, pruning knives, crowns, bells, goblets, spades, sun, moon, stars, butchers' choppers and the tools of many different crafts were all to be found. Certain characteristic local symbols can also be traced. For instance, in St Andrews, the golf club features on the grave of Young Tom Morris. Because names and family details tended to be incised, they were often weathered into illegibility while the aforementioned death symbols, set boldly in high relief, are much better preserved. It's a wee bittie ironic, is it not, that the symbols of death should outlast the details of the individual marked by the stone?

At Dunblane, in the 1600s, a seemingly insoluble dispute between two men over the ownership of a gravestone was cleverly resolved by the Kirk Session who offered it to anyone who would give the kirk treasurer five shillings.

Still to catch on in Scotland is the recent idea of an Austrian company for solar-powered glow-in-the-dark gravestones with a panel where programmable text could be displayed.

TOPPLE TESTING

Victorians loved their monuments to the dead. Even shopkeepers and tradesman aspired to a grand mausoleum in places such as the

Glasgow Necropolis, which opened in the 1830s on the site of the Fir Park, behind Glasgow Cathedral. However substantial and time-less these Greek and Roman follies might seem, they are, in fact, beginning to crumble after a century or more of being exposed to smoke, exhaust pollution and neglect. Because the simple gravestone or the ornate temple of remembrance is the responsibility of the successors of the deceased, local authorities only step in when they are in danger of tumbling. Sadly, the dead are often not long remembered.

With so many monuments now at risk of falling, environmental and civic amenity officials monitor the 'lean' of stones very carefully and, once they are deemed to have become precarious, they are laid flat. A new state-of-the-art sensor to detect the angle and rate of lean is now in the possession of several Scottish local authorities.

TRANSFORMATION

In death, people who were, in truth, ordinary souls can be elevated into icons, famous and revered beyond all reason. Examples of these are plentiful and, in the modern era, we need only to cite the examples of American actress Marilyn Monroe and the cult of Jim Morrison, lead singer of the 1960s band The Doors to make the point. But there are other more subtle, even mystical changes which can result from the change of state from the living to the dead. D J Enright translated a short poem by Raymond Queneau, called 'Conch', which explores this beautifully and concisely:

Living in its shell
the conch never found it easy

to talk to man
now it is dead
it conveys the whole sea to the child's ear
full of wonder
full of wonder

TRANSPORTATION

According to tradition the coffin of St Cuthbert floated down the
Tweed. As Sir Walter Scott relates in 'Marmion':

In his stone coffin forth he rides
(a ponderous bark for river tides),
Yet light as gossamer it glides
Downward to Tillmouth cell.

TREES

The ancient Celts had some interesting coffin traditions. Most
intriguing is the suggestion that coffins – at least of tribal leaders –
were carved from trees planted on the day the deceased was born.

TRIBUTES

When Edinburgh-born inventor Alexander Graham Bell died in
1922, the national telephone services in North America were
suspended for a few minutes in tribute to the man who is credited

with having developed the telephone. A myth grew around this event with such vigour that it is occasionally now suggested that the phone system closed down of its own accord!

Although a proposal to turn off all electric power in the United States for a few minutes, to mark the passing of Scots descendant and electrical genius Thomas Alva Edison, was rejected by Congress, lights nationwide were dimmed briefly on the eve of his funeral.

TWINS

The Siamese twins, Chang and Eng Bunker, who were joined together at the hip for sixty-three years, still managed to sire twenty-one children between them. They died in 1874. Chang became ill and died when Eng slept. When Eng woke, he realised his twin had died, suffered a seizure and died an hour later.

UNDER THE HILL

The man who gave rise to the saying 'away wi' the fairies' was the Rev. Robert Kirk, minister of Aberfoyle in the 1680s. The poor soul is also the one of the best examples of someone who has simply not been allowed to die. A scholarly type with a great love of the Highlands, Kirk published, at Edinburgh in 1684, the first Gaelic version of the Psalms. But there was another, weirder side to his nature – Kirk believed, implicitly, in the existence of fairies. In fact, so entrenched was his belief that he felt compelled to write reams of material about their habits and lifestyle. Among the many characteristics of the fairy folk he described was the fact that they had 'light and changeable bodies of the nature of condensed cloud'. Their voices, it seems, resembled 'whistling', they dwelt under small hillocks and were obliged, for some reason, to change their homes quarterly.

Kirk died suddenly on 14 May 1692, struck down by an 'apoplectic stroke', and expired in the alarmingly precise time, according to observers, of twenty-eight minutes. He was buried in the local kirkyard with a gravestone carrying the inscription 'Robertus Kirk – Linguae Hibernae Lumen'. But was he left to rest in peace with his title of Gaelic Master? No way. So closely had he become associated with the fairies that people just simply refused to accept that he was dead and believed he had been stolen away by the folk who lived under the hill when, in the gloaming, he had accidentally wandered on to a fairy knoll.

A story did the rounds suggesting that Kirk had appeared to a friend with an odd message to the effect that, when Kirk's family were at a baptism, he would appear and, if a knife was thrown over his head, he would be released from the spell and restored to human society. Appear he did, it seems, right on schedule but, for some reason, his cousin, the Laird of Duchray, failed to carry out instructions. You may even find folk in Aberfoyle today who believe that Kirk is in fairyland, slumbering in the illustrious company of the likes of King Arthur and Thomas the Rhymer.

UNDERTAKERS

The job of the undertaker has been described as serving the living by taking care of the dead. You might go as far as to say that funerals are not really for the dead but are a means of indulging the living.

The funeral trade, as we know it in Scotland, only really began at the start of the 1800s. Previously the local joiner would make the coffin and a local housewife, usually a widow and often called the howdie wife in the north, would go to the house of the deceased where she would wash, dress and prepare the body for burial. It's said that, in a few remote areas, this practice was still found in the 1960s.

THE UNDERTAKING BUSINESS

† The Dickensian buildings and the black and purple drapes of pre-war funeral parlours have now largely disappeared in Scotland to be replaced by brighter, airier accommodation.

† The early idea that undertakers belonged to the lower strata of society, almost as if they should be ashamed of their job, has all but disappeared.

† From being regarded as a 'necessary inconvenience', undertakers are now generally seen by the general public as performing a vital function.

† The undertaking business now advertises itself as a promising career prospect for young people with the correct disposition and temperament. Normally employers look for a sense of dedication, empathy and a willingness to serve.

† Recruits tend to be in their twenties with some experience of life and/or other employment. Families of the deceased tend to be more comfortable dealing with more mature young people.

† Up to 900 people are directly employed in the funeral business in Scotland with about 300 firms operating throughout the country. This includes one-person operations, perhaps a carpenter or joiner, in far-flung rural communities where the funeral business might be only one of several occupations for the individual.

† These small businesses are tending to die out amid the welter of EU regulations on freezer storage of bodies and other procedures.

† As part of the modernising of funerals, many businesses organise history boards at funeral services where relatives can pin photographs of the deceased at various stages in their lives.

† Some ten per cent of funerals in Glasgow are now conducted in a humanist/secular style and the number is increasing. This goes hand in hand with the secularisation of society and with the greater involvement of family members – for example, reading the deceased's favourite poems or paying personal tributes.

† Most undertakers see themselves in a shepherding, pastoral role as the new style of funeral begins to unfold. Enabling the family to make informed choices, while ensuring the person is laid to rest with dignity, are keynotes in the advice given.

UNEASINESS

Timor mortis conturbat me.
The fear of death disquiets me.

'Lament for the Makaris'
William Dunbar (1465–1513)

UNFINISHED BUSINESS

A remarkable tale of restlessness after death comes from the Rannoch area. Domhnul Ban a Bhocain, Fair Donald of the Spectre, fought at Culloden and survived the battle. However, within weeks he began to be attacked with stones and mud by an unseen hand although, occasionally, he did see an apparition. Quite naturally, Donald was driven almost to distraction by this constant unseen companion – so much so that he emigrated to America to escape the haunting. However, one day as he walked down a street he saw the spectre approaching him. He returned home, convinced he would be haunted for the rest of his life, before finally plucking up the courage to confront the wraith. The lost soul seemed happy enough to tell his story. Apparently he had fought and fallen by Donald's side at Culloden. He explained that, before joining the Prince's army, he had borrowed a plough from a neighbour and had hidden it beside the Innerchadden Burn. Donald went to the spot, found the plough and informed its owner of its location. The uncanny visitations ceased immediately.

UPLIFTING IDEAS

If we continue to distance ourselves from the dead, will there eventually be a demand for a corporation funeral service in Scotland? Will there come a day when something akin to the cleansing department, but slightly more tasteful, collects the deceased, either at hospital or home, and respectfully disposes of the corpse, thereby preventing the family from ever again having to confront the reality of death? Before you hold up your hands in horror, my straw poll on this idea threw up a surprising number of people who believed it was 'something worth thinking about', especially – and wait for this, you oldies – for grandparents.

Vampires

Think you might be a vampire, the reanimated body of some nasty individual with a crackin' pair of incisors and a passion for opera cloaks? Here is a quick ten-step guide to determine if you are a bloodsucker:

1. Are you a seventh child?
2. Are you over-keen on necking with your partner?
3. Do you have an insatiable longing for black pudding?
4. When the kids ask for a run to the seaside, do you always end up at Slains Castle?
5. Have you always wanted to work with the Scottish Blood Transfusion Service?
6. Do you have a compulsion at karaoke nights to sing 'Fangs for the Memory'?
7. Are you overcritical of people with garlicky breath?
8. Were you born on or near Christmas?
9. When someone mentions 'staking their life' on something, does it send an inexplicable frisson through your chest cavity?
10. Do mirrors and daylight unsettle you?

If you respond positively to up to five of these questions, then there is still hope that you might be plucked from the clutches of the Master. Answer yes to six or more of them and you are spending too much time in that coffin-shaped box in the basement and, for you, life definitely sucks.

VANISHING ACT

Lord Belhaven, pursued by creditors in 1658, arranged his own disappearance. Crossing the Solway Sands, he ordered his servant to return and spread the word that his lordship had been swallowed by the Solway Firth's notorious quicksands. Belhaven then went off to work as a gardener and his wife – who was in on the deception – went into mock mourning. Six years later, when the debts had been cleared, he returned and took up his normal life.

VEILS

There are places throughout Scotland where experts in matters of life and death believe that the veil between this world and the next is at its thinnest. Aberdeenshire author and journalist Norman Adams is one of Scotland's leading ghosts hunters and has written extensively on the subject. After decades of examining strange phenomena across the country, from haunted supermarkets and eerie oil rigs to spooky chapels and council houses, Norman makes a personal selection of Scottish locations where, perhaps, we are at our closest to what lies beyond:

Rosslyn Chapel, Roslin, Midlothian

This medieval building is heavy with psychic atmosphere. Legend tells how a young apprentice mason, who carved the intricate Apprentice Pillar, was murdered by his jealous master. But creepier stories of spectral monks also chill the blood and some visitors have been known to be so scared that they shun the eerie crypt. Motorists in the area should beware too – Gunpowder Brae is haunted by a mounted knight in black.

Warlock Stone, Torphins, Aberdeenshire

Hellfire no longer flickers over Craiglash Hill but it's still not a place to visit after dark. Also known as the 'gryt stane o' Cragleauche', it is mentioned in the Aberdeen Witchcraft Trials of 1596-97 and is the spot where the Deeside coven danced at Hallowe'en as Auld Nick accompanied them on a musical instrument. After the trials, the women were burned at the stake. To this day, folk claim there is no birdsong in daytime here.

Dunnottar Castle, near Stonehaven

Stand facing this dark ruined fortress as a gale lashes its sea-girt rock and you cannot fail to be overawed by its grim history. The Whigs' Vault is testimony of the suffering imposed on 167 Covenanters, including forty-two women, who were tortured and starved while imprisoned in filthy and cramped conditions in 1685. In desperation, two men perished when they attempted to escape down the rockface. Visitors who have experienced the castle ghosts reported them to be a phantom girl, a guard and a deerhound. Eerie voices coming from a meeting in the unoccupied gatehouse, known as Benholm's Lodging, have also been heard.

MARY KING'S CLOSE, EDINBURGH

This narrow old close under the City Chambers in High Street is said to be the most haunted place in Auld Reekie. It's certainly a Mecca for tourists in search of spooks. An old generation referred to the area as the 'plague toon' because pestilence wiped out the residents in 1645. A ghost girl and her dog have been reported but most tourists find the bizarre shrine to her memory – a kind of cairn comprised of dolls, sweets, postcards and coins deposited by visitors – particularly haunting.

FYVIE CASTLE, ABERDEENSHIRE

The charter room is said to be the coldest room in the castle and, when I was invited there after visiting hours, the lights inexplicably failed! My guide explained how people grow uncomfortable when entering the room. Other ghostly horrors include the Green Lady – whose sudden appearance was said to be a harbinger of death – a cold hand that roused guests, phantom footsteps, the cursed 'Weeping Stones' and indelible bloodstains on the floor of the former 'Murder Room', a favourite haunt of the Green Lady. Warning – don't get locked in!

VENGEANCE

Malcolm's Point on the east coast of the Ross of Mull is a 1,000-foot high headland which recalls a quite horrendous story of man's inhumanity to man. Malcolm Gorry was a deerstalker for the Chief of Loch Buie. When he failed in his allotted task of guarding a certain pass during a hunt, thereby allowing the deer to escape, Loch

Buie ordered Malcolm to be bound and severely whipped, whereupon the stalker vowed immediate and dreadful vengeance. As soon as he was loose he sprang for the laird's son and threatened to throw the boy off the cliff. Loch Buie was distraught with grief and agreed to be flogged as Malcolm had been. Still the stalker refused to hand over the boy, demanding that the chief suffer mutilation. As soon as that demand had been meted out, Gorry grasped the child tightly and leaped out into the abyss, taking the boy with him.

WAKES OR LYKEWAKES

The chamber of death in the 1600s and 1700s was not the sombre, dark and cold place that the modern imagination conjures up. It was a curious mixture of the sacred and the profane, filled night after night with laughter, bible readings, song and story, the music of the fiddle and the pipes and the clatter of reels. It was generally styled a lykewake, the lyke being the corpse and the wake, the watch over the body.

Much as the Reformed Church attempted to curtail these unseemly and boisterous activities, from the mid 1500s, they persisted into the first half of the nineteenth century. Under the Victorian influence, excessive feasting, drinking and the inevitable scrapping all but ceased and people began to take a much more serious, responsible view of the rituals of death.

Weird occurrences at these earlier wakes can often be explained by the vast quantities of drink consumed. Hide-and-seek was a popular pastime at the wake, some of the competitors being happy to climb into bed with the corpse in the quest for a secure hidey-hole. Wakes originated in the custom of watching through the night to say prayers for the soul of the dead. Refreshment naturally had to

261

be offered and it seems that, in time, this evolved into a sort of party.

However, once the partying started, it became very quickly established as the norm. According to David Grewar, these events were so much enjoyed that 'not infrequently the death of somebody who had lingered o'er long was anticipated with much impatience'.

An interesting lykewake ruse is described by Christine Quigley. After the limbs of an arthritic body were tied down to straighten them for the wake, a practical joker would, from time to time, cut the ropes causing the body to sit bold upright in the midst of the festivities. If a game of cards were played around the coffin, the deceased would either be dealt a hand or used as a gaming table – or both.

WAR

Scottish losses during the two World Wars of the twentieth century amounted to 148,115 in the First World War and 57,684 in the Second.

WARNINGS

The importance of family life in late fifteenth-century Scotland is shown by an incident when man of the house Thomson Lorn was brought before the Provost of Aberdeen after being posted missing for seven weeks. He was warned that he would suffer the death penalty if he abandoned his family again without warning. The scariest aspect of this story is surely the fact that the Provost of the

Granite City had the power of life and death over the citizens. A return to such executive power might slow the boy racers on the Beach Boulevard down a bittie.

WATERY ENDS

As late as the mid 1600s, death by drowning for theft was still applied in Scotland.

WAYS TO BE OFFENSIVE AT FUNERALS

1. Listen to the *Sportsound* football commentary on your headphones during the 'Twenty-Third Psalm'
2. Hand out rear-end views of the deceased created on the office photocopier and then ask someone to photograph you shaking hands with the deceased
3. Turn up at the funeral wearing a Tony Blair (or George W Bush) mask or a Count Dracula outfit.
4. Shake the widow's hand with an electric buzzer and tell her the deceased's last wish was that she should marry you
5. Tell the clergyman that the deceased is one of the undead and ask permission to drive a stake through his heart
6. Send the widow a gothic strippergram the day after the funeral
7. At the cemetery casually ask about the frequency of premature burial and suggest that the body should be stuffed rather than buried.

WEATHER

Weather-induced death through hypothermia or, less often, through heatstroke is clearly a factor in Scotland's mortality figures. However, it seems from the following old saw that certain types of conditions are kinder:

Frosty winter, misty spring, chequered summer and sunny autumn,
Never left death in Scotland.

WEEPING AND WAILING

Sir Walter Scott promised that, for ages to come, we would, as a nation, 'wail' over the outcome of the Battle of Flodden in September 1513, when King James IV and most of his nobility perished. The effect on the nation was devastating. One nineteenth-century genealogist noted, 'The more I look into any Scottish charter chest, the more I am sensibly struck; almost every distinguished Scottish family having then been prematurely deprived of an ancestor or a member.' A time for wailing, indeed.

WEIGHT OF A SOUL

Scientists who have tried to argue the existence of a soul say the body, immediately post-mortem, can have mysteriously lost up to an ounce and a half in weight. That sounds gey like heavy soul tae me, man.

Well of Seven Heads

At Invergarry, there is a monument commemorating one of the deeds of blood for which the Highlands are famous – or infamous. At the foot of the monument, a little spring of clear, cold water bubbles. The top of the shaft of the monument is crowned by a hand grasping seven heads transfixed by a dagger. The story goes that two young chiefs of Keppoch were murdered after returning from education on the continent and deciding to 'drive all thieves and cattle lifters' from their corner of Lochaber. The chieftain of one of the minor branches of the clan resented this intrusion into local custom and practice and, with his six sons, he waded across the River Spean and murdered the young chief in his bed, before slaying his younger brother who came to his aid.

The poet Ian Lom, the biting bard of Keppoch, railed against the murderers – especially when it became clear that Glengarry, the superior of Clan Donald, was unlikely to make any official retribution. Sir James McDonald of Sleat in Skye despatched a party of islemen up the valley of the Spean to Inverlair where they surprised the father and six sons in bed. The house was set on fire and the six young men were dragged outside and dirked to death. But the shout went up, 'The six cubs are here but the old fox is still in his den.' He was hauled from the burning house and done to death.

The bard then severed the heads and put them in a sack, making off on a circuitous route to Invergarry for a confrontation with Glengarry. Before reaching the castle, tradition has it that he washed the heads in the spring. At his meeting with the chief he taunted Glengarry with sarcasm over his failure to avenge the death of a kinsman, albeit distant, and laid the heads at Glengarry's feet. They were later buried in a glade near the mansion house of Invergarry.

There are several little twists to this gory tale. The mother of the assassins who killed the young chief and his brother was Lom's sister. The monument was erected in 1812 by Colonel M'Donnell, last chief of Glengarry, and the mound at Inverlair where the bodies were supposed to have been buried was excavated by a nosy Victorian antiquarian. He found seven skeletons in the earth. The skeletons were complete – except they each lacked a skull. Seldom are the traditional stories of the Scottish Highlands confirmed in such a dramatic manner.

WILLS

It's definitely a good idea to get all your affairs sorted out before you snuff out life's candle – it saves the relatives indulging in internecine warfare for the next half-century. Apart from that, it also offers you an opportunity to strike from the grave – somewhere they'll have difficulty getting back at you.

> And to my wife who always said she adored my cheery smile, I leave my dentures.

Such were the dangers and uncertainties of travelling to the wild and woolly south in the seventeenth and eighteenth century that many Highlanders and Islanders had their wills written up in advance of the journey.

WITCHES

Witches in Scotland were often considered to be bringers of death – either through conjured illnesses or as storm-raisers or wreckers. The famous coven of witches at North Berwick was accused of attempting to deal death to James VI and his bride Anne as they entered the Forth on their return from Denmark, by sinking their ship through casting spells.

The favourite tool of Highland witches was a voodoo-style clay body made from unfired clay. It was often left in a stream and, as the water eroded its substance, the victim slowly wasted away.

WOLVES AND DUGS

During the 1400s, a number of reports from the Highlands suggested that rampaging packs of wolves had been digging up newly buried corpses. The current legislation for burial in Scotland is some 150 years old (The Burial Grounds (Scotland) Act of 1855) but there is little to dictate the minimum depth for human remains. Indeed, while the rules for the disposal of deceased cattle are staggeringly comprehensive, those governing the human equivalent are sparse. This leaves burial authorities with a degree of freedom in the matter. One exasperated West of Scotland council official, when endlessly pressed by a diligent councillor on the minimum depth for burials, declared that it should be at least sufficient to 'keep the dugs fae the bones'.

WOMEN

In the Highlands, it was not the custom for women to follow the funeral – although, in some areas, they might carry the coffin for the first few yards. Prior to the nineteenth century, women might go as far as the first burn where, after partaking of a 'light refreshment', they returned while the cortege proceeded on its way. On the day after the funeral, many of the women of the district gathered to 'tramp' the blankets from the bed on which the deceased had expired. Drink was again supplied, for these ladies liked a swallie, and occasionally sprained ankles and even broken bones resulted from their enthusiastic post-funeral activities.

WOODWORM

Of all the many scores of death omens which the Scots thought they had identified over the centuries, probably the most widely found was the clicking noise made by the woodworm. This chilling sound, redolent of dark earth and last resting places, still has the power to remind us of our mortality.

WORDS

Shaking hands and attempting a few words of comfort to the bereaved is perhaps the most difficult moment at funerals. We want to empathise but it is difficult to find the correct words. Despite our best intentions we stumble in our attempts to reach out. A straw poll suggests that these are the most common expressions of sympathy uttered as the flesh is pressed:

1. I'm so sorry
2. God bless
3. We're all thinking of you
4. It was probably for the best
5. You can think about a fresh start
6. It must be such a relief
7. He/she was a fine man/woman
8. If only . . .
9. If there's anything we can do to help . . .
10. I just don't know what to say

Spoken over the coffin at countless millions of funerals have been these words:

> Man that is born of woman hath but a short time to live and is full of misery. He cometh up and is cut down like a flower; he fleeth as it were a shadow, and never continueth in one stay.

X-RATED

It's not just on the top shelves of the local newspaper/magazine shops that Scotsmen can encounter X-rated material. A few years back *Men's Health* magazine scared the beejesus out of the dying Scot with its 'Stay Alive in 2001 Calendar'. The January and February illustrations depicted car crashes while March and April cheerfully moved along to portray lung cancer. Other joys hidden in the year ahead included liver disease, suicide and digestive disorders. As one columnist observed, 'Just the thing to brighten up the wall.'

YOUNG FOLK

If and when young people contemplate death, the carbolic, hospitalised death seems the most alarming option. If it has to be, then going out spectacularly is the priority.

Liverpool poet Roger McGough got to grips with this philosophy in the splendid wee poem 'Let Me Die a Young Man's Death', the second stanza of which runs:

> When I'm 73
> and in constant good tumour
> may I be mown down at dawn
> by a bright red sports car
> on my way home from an all-night party.

The obsession with youthfulness, with staying young, cultivated by the media and encouraged by advertisers, means that those who are old and sick are sidelined. However, as has often been said, death is the one certainty in all our lives, old and young. Undertaker Dominic Maguire observes that, while we happily fork out for car insurance, house insurance and the like, there is a lack of preparedness for the one event for which there is no escape – and deep unwillingness even to think about the practical implications of death. Would it be valuable to include death, funerals and the emotions surrounding bereavement as part of life skills classes? Dominic Maguire certainly believes so.

ZOMBIES

These might be seen as spiritless bodies that appear to be out to make life as miserable as possible for everyone else – even when limbs have been lopped off or they have been gassed, shot, knifed, incinerated, buried, melted, run over, on they press.

It is said that zombies, still a feature of life in Haiti it seems, were raised by magicians and, if fed salt, would turn on their master before returning to the grave. More recent theories suggest that the zombie is someone who has been drugged and controlled by a powerful, even charismatic, individual. One technique to get rid of these party-poopers might be to force them to watch endless repeats of *Night of the Living Dead*.

AFTERTHOUGHT

At the age of fifty-six I am nearer, much nearer it sometimes feels, to the end of my life than to the beginning. Over these decades, I can reflect on so much happiness and pain.

As far as genuinely close encounters with death – at least those that I know about – are concerned, there have been only two. In the early 1970s, I came close when a burst ulcer left me within minutes of death. The skill of the surgeons at Glasgow's Western Infirmary brought me back from the edge. I remember, or think I remember, floating about the operating theatre, free as a bird . . . eerily seeing myself on the operating table. Was this as a result of the anaesthetic kicking in or loss of blood – or was it a genuine near-death experience? Who knows?

In the same decade, on a Paris boulevard, a saloon car, driven by a druggie, impaled itself at high speed on the other side of a stepped stone traffic bollard only feet from where my wife Morag and I were standing waiting to cross. Our only injuries were tiny lacerations caused by showers of shattered stone and glass. It was the closest of calls.

As a result of these experiences, I have only one observation and one plea to make. The observation is the strange sensation that I had, on both of these occasions, of seeming to have stepped out of time with events. It appeared to take both forever and an instant to negotiate these experiences. Clumsily put, I know, but that was how it felt – and I have no idea what it means. And my plea is that you enjoy your life – with every ounce of your being, enjoy it.

J H

BIBLIOGRAPHY

GENERAL

Abbott, Geoffrey, *The Book of Execution* (London: Headline, 1994)

Enright, D J (ed.), *The Oxford Book of Death* (Oxford: Oxford University Press, 1983)

Gorer, Geoffrey, *Death, Grief and Mourning in Contemporary Britain* (London: Cresset Publishing, 1965)

Litten, Julian, *The English Way of Death* (London: Robert Hale, 1991)

Lynch, Thomas, *The Undertaking* (London: Jonathan Cape, 1997)

Palmer, Greg, *Death: The Trip of a Lifetime* (New York: Diane Publishing Co., 1993)

Parkes, Colin Murray, Pittu Laungani and Bill Young (eds), *Death and Bereavement Across Cultures* (London: Routledge, 1996)

Quigley, Christine, *The Corpse – A History* (North Carolina: McFarland and Company, 1996)

Tibballs, Geoff, *Unbelievable Facts* (Bath: Parragon, 2000)

SCOTTISH

Adams, Norman, *Haunted Scotland* (Edinburgh: Mainstream, 1998)

Ballingal, James, *The Rhynd and Elcho – A Parish History* (Edinburgh: 1905)

Barr, W T, *For a Web Begun – The Story of Dunfermline* (Edinburgh: 1947)

Barron, E M, *Inverness in the Fifteenth Century* (Inverness: 1906)

Barty, Alexander (ed.), *The History of Dunblane* (Stirling: Stirling Council Libraries, 1944)

Beveridge, David, *Culross and Tulliallan or Perthshire on the Forth – Its History and Antiquities, Vol. II,* (Edinburgh: 1885)

Chambers, Robert, *Domestic Annals of Scotland* (Edinburgh: 1861)

Cunningham, A, S, *Dysart: Past and Present* (Leven: 1912)

Dick, R, *Annals of Colinsburgh* (Edinburgh: 1896)

Donaldson, Gordon and Robert S Morpeth (eds), *A Dictionary of Scottish History* (Edinburgh: John Donald, 1977).

Dunnett, Hamilton, *Invera'an – A Strathspey Parish* (Paisley: 1919)

Fergusson, R Menzies, *Logie – A Parish History, Vol. I,* (Paisley: 1905)

Fittis, Robert Scott, *Sketches in Olden Times in Perthshire* (Perth: 1878)

Forrester, Rev. David Marshall, *Logiealmond* (Edinburgh: 1944)

Fraser, Alexander, *Tayvallich and North Knapdale* (Glasgow: John Smith, 1962)

Fraser-Mackintosh, Charles, *Antiquarian Notes, Historical, Genealogical and Social (Second Series) Inverness-shire Parish by Parish* (Inverness: 1897)

Gordon, Anne, *Death Is for the Living* (Edinburgh: Harris Publishing, 1984)

Gordon, Anne, 'Death and Burial', in Michael Lynch (ed.), *The Oxford Companion to Scottish History* (Oxford: Oxford University Press, 2001)

Grewar, David, *The Story of Glenisla* (Aberdeen: 1926)

Hay, George, *History of Arbroath* (Arbroath: 1899)

Henderson, Robert, *Scottish Keeriosities* (Edinburgh: Saint Andrew Press, 1995)

Houston, Archibald, *Auchterderran – A Parish History* (Paisley: 1924)

Inglis, W Mason, *Annals of an Angus Parish – Auchterhouse* (SW Forfarshire) (Dundee: 1888)

Jillings, Karen, *Scotland's Black Death* (Stroud: Tempus Publishing, 2002)

Kirk, Russell, *St Andrews* (London: 1954)

Loder, John De Vere, *Colonsay and Oronsay in the Isles of Argyll* (Edinburgh: Colonsay Press, 1935)

Macara, A, *Crieff – Its Traditions and Characters* (Edinburgh: 1881)

Macdonald, Andrew Joseph, *Glen Albyn or Tales and Truths of the Central Highlands*, (Fort Augustus: Abbey Press, 1920)

Mackay, William, *Urquhart and Glenmoriston – Olden Times in a Highland Parish* (Inverness: 1914)

Mackenzie, William, *Skye* (Glasgow: 1930)

Maclagan, Bessie, *Madderty – A Short History of an Ancient Parish* (Perth: 1933)

Maclean, J P, *History of the Island of Mull* (Ohio: 1923)

MacLeod, Donald, *Ancient Records of Dumbarton* (Dumbarton: 1896)

Macmillan, Somerled, *Bygone Lochaber* (Glasgow: Caledonian Books, 1971)

Malcolm, J, *The Parish of Monifeith in Ancient and Modern Times* (Edinburgh: 1910)

Marwick, Ernest, *The Folklore of Orkney and Shetland* (London: Rowman and Littlefield, 1975)

Melville, Lawrence, *Errol: Its Legends, Lands and People* (Perth: Culross, 1935)

Paton, Henry (ed.), *Register of Internments in the Greyfriars Burying Ground, Edinburgh 1658–1700* (Edinburgh: 1902)

Ross, William, *Aberdour and Inchcolme* (Edinburgh: 1885)

Ross, William (ed.), *John Blaine's History of Bute* (Rothesay: 1880)

Spence, Alan, *Way to Go* (London: MacAdam/Cage Publishing, 1998)

Stewart, Alexander, *A Highland Parish or the History of Fortingall* (Glasgow: 1928)

Swire, Otta F, *The Outer Hebrides and their Legends* (Edinburgh: Oliver & Boyd, 1966)

Walker, Colin, *Scottish Proverbs* (Edinburgh: Birlinn, 2000)